UNLEASHED TEMPTATION

MIAMI SCORCHER SERIES

Savannah Stuart

Cover art: Jaycee of Sweet 'N Spicy Designs
Author website: www.savannahstuartauthor.com

Unleashed Temptation/KR Press, LLC -- 1st ed.

ISBN-10: 1942447205
ISBN-13: 9781942447207

eISBN: 9781942447191

Praise for the books of Savannah Stuart

"Fans of sexy paranormal romance should definitely treat themselves to this sexy & fun story." —Nina's Literary Escape

"I enjoyed this installment so much I'll be picking up book one...worth the price for the punch of plot and heat." —Jessie, HEA USA Today blog

"...a scorching hot read." —The Jeep Diva

"This story was a fantastic summer read!" —Book Lovin' Mamas

"If you're looking for a hot, sweet read, be sure not to miss Tempting Alibi. It's one I know I'll revisit again and again." —Happily Ever After Reviews

"You will not regret reading the previous story or this one. I would recommend it to anyone who loves a great shifter story." —The Long & Short of It

"…a fun and sexy shapeshifter book and definitely worth the read." —The Book Binge

"I'm going to need a bigger moving trailer." Carly Kendall entered her bedroom carrying another empty moving box.

Stacie, Carly's best friend of fifteen years and roommate of four, shook her head as she grabbed the box from her. "What you need is a sexy man in your bed."

Carly rolled her eyes and picked up a handful of thick, winter scarves from the floor. That was Stacie's answer to everything. "No, what I *need* is a change of scenery. I'm tired of Chicago and I'm tired of this weather. Miami is the perfect place for a new start. Sunny weather year round."

"What about hurricanes?"

Carly shrugged and dumped her handful on the bed. "Better than snowstorms and blackouts."

Stacie sat on the edge of Carly's bed and held up the scarves. "What do you want me to do with these?"

"Keep half of them and put the rest in the box marked winter clothes. I won't need them where

I'm going." She grinned at her friend as she turned back toward her closet.

"And this has nothing to do with that snake Dan?" Stacie asked.

Carly turned to find her friend digging through her jewelry. "Hey, I said you could take some scarves, not half my room... And no, this has nothing to do with him."

"Hmm." Stacie avoided her gaze as she opened a drawer and dumped it into one of the boxes.

Carly cringed at her friend's lack of organization. She'd be digging through boxes for days trying to figure out what went where. "Okay, maybe it has a little to do with him, but a lot to do with the fact that I need to mix it up. I don't have any family here—"

"Hey!" The hurt look on Stacie's face made Carly cringe.

"I didn't mean it like that. You know you're like family to me. It's just...I don't know, I need something different right now. I can't explain it." Sighing, she flopped down on her bed. Finding out her boyfriend—now ex-boyfriend—had been cheating on her hadn't bothered her much. That was a sign in itself that she should have broken up with Dan months ago. Hell, with their conflicting schedules they hadn't had sex in over four months. And they hadn't had *good* sex in she couldn't remember how long.

The only thing that pissed her off was that he'd been screwing *her* boss. Certainly explained all that overtime she'd been roped into doing. At least she had a nice savings account. She wasn't worried about finding work, and now she'd have time to relax and learn her way around the city before job hunting. Not to mention she planned to hit the beach as soon as she got there.

"Fine, I guess I understand. But I reserve the right to come visit you anytime."

"As if that was ever an issue. You better come visit me."

"I can't believe you're living with your grand-mother." Stacie snickered as she dumped the con-tents of another drawer into the same box.

Carly jumped off the bed and scooted her friend out of the way with her hip. "How about you stick with boxing my clothes and I'll take over this dress-er... And, I'm not living with her. I'm living in the apartment behind her house."

"Same thing," Stacie mumbled.

It wasn't, but Carly didn't correct her. She knew her friend was bummed she was leaving and the truth was, Stacie was the only reason she'd even contemplated staying in Chicago in the first place. Carly's grandmother had moved to Florida two years ago and she'd almost left then, but back then she'd loved her job and friends. She still loved her friends, but it was time to take control of her life. She had no desire to get stagnant or settled.

As she unhooked a string of beads she and Stacie had gotten at the last St. Patrick's Day parade, an unexpected wave of emotions threatened to overwhelm her. She really was going to miss Stacie. "You want to put off packing and head to Cullen's Bar for happy hour?"

Stacie swiveled from the closet. She dropped the bundle of shirts in her hand and grinned. "Hell yeah."

Carly pulled the ponytail holder from her hair and gave herself a quick glance in the mirror. One night of partying with her friend wouldn't make a difference in how soon she got to Miami.

* * *

Two Weeks Later

Scrubbing a hand over his face, Nick Lazos sank into his comfortable chair with a sigh. He turned on his computer and sat back, waiting for it to start. After the last disastrous interview, he seriously hoped he had some new responses to his want ad. He couldn't keep doing all this admin stuff on top of everything else.

When there was a soft knock at his office door he glanced at the wall clock. Inwardly he groaned. Even though he needed a new accountant, he'd been hoping the last interviewee wouldn't show up today. His mother had talked him into interviewing one of her friend's granddaughters. If she was anything like the last woman his mom had recommended—he fought off a shudder.

"Come in," he barked. Better get this over with.

The door creaked open and for a moment, he forgot to breathe. This could *not* be the woman here to interview.

A pretty redhead took a couple tentative steps inside. Her ivory cheeks were flushed a delectable shade of pink. "Hi, I'm Carly Kendall. I hope I'm not late."

Somehow he found his voice. "You're right on time." Instinctively he stood and motioned for her to sit across the desk. Now he wished he'd taken a few minutes to straighten up.

She wore a respectable dark blue pencil skirt and button-down blouse, but the effect on her was 'naughty librarian'. Which was the last thing he should be thinking about. The shape of her perfect-ly rounded breasts pressed against her top and all he could think about doing was unbuttoning it and peeling it open slowly, inch by inch, as her delectable body was revealed to him.

What the *fuck* was wrong with him? He mentally shook himself, needing to get his shit together.

He wasn't some horny fucking adolescent, but something about her scent was making him crazy. It was unusual, like a spring rain and a hint of raspberries— Crap, she was saying something.

"I appreciate you taking the time to interview me. I wasn't sure if you had it so here's my résumé." She slid it across the desk as she spoke.

"Why don't you tell me a little about yourself and why you want to work here?" There, he got out a coherent sentence. He deserved a freaking medal for being able to talk when she was staring at him with those big blue eyes, begging him to do all sorts of bad things. Damn, he could practically feel his canines extending. As a werewolf, he'd learned to control his urges as a pup. For some reason, his primal instinct was overruling all those ingrained rules. When she nervously moistened her lips he realized he was staring a little too hard.

Nick quickly glanced at her résumé. "Finance?" Good for him. Another word. He looked up again.

A real smile touched her shiny pink, oh-so-kissable lips. "Yes. After college I started working at..."

Oh shit. Shit, shit, shit! He'd always had a thing for redheads. Funny that he'd never dated one, but especially not a human one. And now his living, breathing fantasy wanted to work for him. She wasn't glamorous or exotic—*or a shifter*—but she was *exactly* his type. Something he hadn't realized he even had until she'd walked through the door of his office. Adorable freckles splattered her nose and cheeks, giving her an innocent quality he usually detested.

He wanted a woman with experience. Too bad his dick had other plans. It had taken one look at sexy Ms. Kendall and gone on red alert. What *the fuck* was wrong with him? He'd been in her presence sixty seconds and he felt like one of his barbaric ancestors, ready to take her back to his cave and claim her. Hell, maybe his ancestors had been on to something because that sounded like a damn good idea.

"And with five years of experience I think I can be a great asset to your company." She sat there staring at him expectantly.

What had she been saying? Was she expecting a response? He cleared his throat and glanced down at her résumé, mainly so he wouldn't freak her out by staring. She certainly had the right work history. More than enough to do this job. Dealing with his roughneck employees is what had caused the last assistant to leave though. Of course, she'd had a permanent stick up her ass so he'd been happy to see that one go even if she had left him high and dry.

"Mr. Lazos?" Carly—Ms. Kendall—crossed her toned legs and bit her bottom lip.

She stared at him with those intoxicating eyes and he knew he needed to say something. Anything. Before the words were out, he was completely aware he was going to regret this, but what choice did he have. He didn't have time to go through a dozen more interviews and she had more than enough qualifications. Not to mention, viable candidates weren't banging down the door to work here. So what if he ended up walking around with a permanent hard-on. He'd get used to it.

He cleared his throat. "This all looks very impressive. If you started here, you'd be in charge of payroll and handle all the accounting for this shop and the other two I own. I have about forty-five employees, but I plan to expand soon. Do you think that's something you could handle?"

Smiling, she nodded. "At my last job I handled the payroll for close to two hundred people and I'm a certified CPA so I could take care of all your taxes at the end of the year too."

Turning her down simply because she made him hot would be a mistake. Carly Kendall was a dream employee. She had all the qualifications and then some. And... he didn't want to let her walk out that door without knowing he'd see her again. "I pay bi-weekly and if it works out, after thirty days you get medical and dental, two weeks paid vacation, and ten paid sick days." He rattled off the salary and when she blinked, he knew she'd take the job if he offered it.

"Can you start this week?" he managed to choke out.

Her gorgeous blue eyes widened as if that had been the last thing she'd expected. Her mouth dropped open for a fraction of a second before she contained herself. "Yes, of course. Tomorrow, if you want. Uh, don't you want to check my references?"

Good God, where was his head? "I plan to make the necessary calls today. If there's a problem, I'll contact you. If not, I'll see you tomorrow."

"Wonderful." She smiled, revealing a perfect row of white teeth. The pleasure rolling off her was sweet and palpable.

His heart rate kicked up about a thousand degrees. "Be here at nine." He gritted his teeth and tried to discreetly shift in his seat. His cock pressed painfully against the zipper of his pants.

"What exactly is the dress code here?"

"Dress code?" He stared dumbly at her.

"Well, I know the mechanics wear...uh, coveralls, or whatever those things are called, but what do I wear?"

"The last assistant I had wore skirts and dresses. Nothing fancy though." He bit back the momentary twinge of guilt as she nodded enthusiastically. His last assistant had worn jeans and polo T-shirts. It was an auto shop for God's sake. The customers didn't give a shit what they wore so long as they fixed their cars and didn't rip them off. Nick, however, wanted to see those long legs again so he flat-out lied.

"Great. Well if that's all, I guess I'll see you tomorrow morning. Thank you for this opportunity, Mr. Lazos." She stood and held out a slim, elegant hand.

He stared at it for a moment before grasping it in his much bigger one. He started to stand then stopped himself. If he did, she'd no doubt see his reaction to her and run for the hills. Then he'd have to start the interview process all over again. "See you tomorrow. And call me Nick," he said before blindly picking up a stack of papers and purposely ignoring her.

As soon as the door shut behind her he let out a long breath and let his head fall against the desk. "You are an idiot," he muttered to himself.

Seconds later the door swung open, interrupting his internal curses.

"Who was the cute redhead?" Jimmy, one of his mechanics asked.

"She's the new office manager."

Jimmy's lusty grin grew wider and Nick could smell the man's arousal as it rolled over the room. Hell, even without his extrasensory abilities, he knew exactly what the man was thinking—because he was thinking it too. "She's the most qualified applicant we've had and she's off limits. To you, to everyone. Spread it around because she starts to-morrow."

Jimmy held up his hands in mock defense and the lust Nick had smelled dissipated almost immediately. "Calm down, boss. All I said was she was cute. I'll let everyone know."

"Good. And watch your fucking language around her too!" Carly had class written all over her and he didn't want his guys running her off.

Not bothering to hide his laughter, Jimmy shut the door behind him on his way out.

Nick looked around his office and cringed. Stacks of paper were everywhere, and a dirty carburetor sat on one of the shelves. The room hadn't been cleaned in—hell, he couldn't remember how long. Muttering to himself, he started straightening up. Technically it was his office, but she'd be using it the majority of the day and he wanted it to be comfortable for her.

As he moved around the small room, his body tensed. Her raspberry scent lingered in the air, assaulting all his senses and making his wolf agitated, hungry. His entire body tensed as his canines extended. Unless he was being threatened, he normally had complete control over his body. Taking a few calming breaths, he sat and clutched the armrest of his chair until the threat of change subsided.

CHAPTER TWO

Nick jerked upright in bed, his breathing erratic. A light sheen of sweat covered his neck and
chest. He scrubbed a hand over his face and shook
his head, trying to clear the cobwebs of sleep. Yesterday had been long as hell and it felt like he'd *just*
dozed off.

For a second he was disoriented until he spotted
the digital clock on his nightstand. Time to get
ready for work. As he swung his legs off the bed, he
groaned when his sheet rubbed against his rock-
hard cock.

He shoved the thin cover off himself and headed
for the bathroom, acutely aware of the aching between his legs. The tile cooled his feet but it did little to cool the memories of the particularly erotic
dream he'd been having about Carly.

She'd been on his mind since yesterday. He'd
thought about her on the drive home, *at* home, and
when his head had hit the pillow last night.

As he drew the shower curtain back and turned
on the water, his other hand automatically fisted

around his cock. It was as if his hand had a mind of its own. Maybe he should be embarrassed to fantasize about Carly while getting off, but damn, he couldn't get the vixen out of his head.

He'd spoken to her for all of twenty minutes and he was waking up with a hard-on for her. He couldn't remember the last time he'd actually dreamt about a woman not featured in a magazine. Now he was waking up panting like some randy pup. Sure, it had been a while since he'd had sex, but not so long that he should be acting like this.

As he stepped under the powerful jet stream, he started working his fist in long, fluid motions. Images of working Carly into a sexual frenzy entered his mind unbidden and all his senses heightened.

He could practically smell her sweet raspberry scent surrounding him as if she were standing right in front of him. Hell, if she was here right now, he'd kiss and taste every inch of her body until she was wet and begging for him. The overwhelming need to dominate her shouldn't surprise him, but it did.

What he wanted from her was different than anything he'd experienced and he barely knew the woman. As his free hand pressed against the tile to support himself, her face swam before him, taunting him, teasing him.

What he wouldn't give to feel her nails dig into his back or to taste between her legs. He could just imagine stroking his tongue along her slick folds.

At the sound of the metal hooks scraping against the shower rod, Nick's eyes flew open. His shoulders tensed but before he could react, the curtain was drawn back and in stepped Carly.

Completely naked.

For a moment, he forgot to breathe. Pale pink nipples were barely visible underneath the long hair cascading over her chest and a soft tuft of fine, red hair covered her mound.

He automatically reached out to touch her. Where, it didn't matter. He simply needed his hands on her.

In the recesses of his mind, reality screamed at him and his hand froze. What the hell was going on? This was definitely a dream. He shook his head, uncaring. If it was, he didn't want to wake up.

"What are you doing here?" he rasped out.

"Shh." She pressed a long finger to his lips before drawing the curtain back into place.

She turned to face him and her eyes darkened as they roved over his body. His cock jerked under her scrutiny. It felt like a heavy club between his legs and she was the only woman who could relieve him.

With a trembling hand, he pushed aside any thoughts that this might be a dream and reached out to touch her smooth skin. Her waist was slim but her hips flared out into perfect curves. Just enough for him to grasp onto as he pounded into her.

Or as she rode him. Either way, it didn't matter as long as his cock was inside her.

Wordlessly, she stepped toward him, pressing her luscious body against the full length of his. He was aware of water rushing over them, but the main thing he felt was her hard nipples brushing against his chest.

As she moved against him, the pebbles teased his skin. Nick shuddered as their bodies connected. Unable to stand it anymore and not caring if this was a fantasy he'd concocted, he threaded his fingers through her thick hair and slanted his mouth over hers.

Damn, the woman even tasted like raspberries. Sweet and succulent. He groaned into her mouth as he imagined licking her pussy. His tongue stroked inside her as he cupped her head tightly. If he were a betting man, he'd guess she tasted just as sweet between her legs.

At that thought, his other hand strayed lower. If he couldn't taste her, he'd settle for second best. Normally he liked to explore all of a woman's body before making a break straight for her pussy, but he couldn't wait. The need to touch her most intimate area was overwhelming.

Cupping her soft mound, he slid his middle finger over her clit and between her folds. At that, her body jolted against his. It was slight, but he could feel the ripple straight to where their mouths were connected.

Just as he suspected, she was tight. Her inner walls clamped around his finger as he slowly inserted it. Dragging his finger back out, he ran it over her clit, covering the sensitive area with her own slickness.

"Ahh." She let out a tiny moan against him.

"Do you like that?" he murmured against her mouth in between kisses.

Her answer wasn't audible, but she nodded her approval.

Taking a chance, he eased another finger inside her and was rewarded by a surprised gasp. For a split second he paused, wondering if he'd hurt her, but when her hips surged forward, he pushed deeper.

She clutched at his shoulders and he increased his movement between her legs. Not too fast, but a steady rhythm. In and out, nice and slow. If the way her body trembled under his touch was any indication, she was close to climaxing.

Hell, he was close to coming and she was barely touching him.

With each stroke, he pressed his fingers against her inner walls, loving the way her tight body clenched around him.

Unable to stand just feeling her aroused nipples against his chest anymore, he released his grip from her head and reached between their bodies to cup her breast. His hands were callused from work but she didn't seem to notice.

When he rubbed the pad of his thumb across her distended nipple, her hips gave an erratic jerk against his other hand.

"I take it you like that too," he whispered as he feathered a few more kisses along her jaw.

"Don't stop." Her voice was ragged and unsteady.

Though he didn't want to pull away from kissing her, he knelt down and gently flicked her clit with his tongue.

She was taller than average for a woman, but everything about her was delicate. Long arms, long legs, and he didn't want to do anything to hurt the soft folds between those legs.

Her knees trembled so she leaned back against the tiled wall, using it as support. The position was perfect for what he wanted.

He could feel how close she was. With each stroke, her tight sheath clenched around his fingers. She just needed the right stimulation. When he sucked on her clit; that was all it took for her to lose control. Her hands gripped his head as her inner walls spasmed around him.

As she rode through the last surge of her climax, the jerky movements of her hips subsided until she was simply trembling against the wall. Her hands fell away from him and when he looked up at her, her lips were parted slightly in bliss.

He stood, ready to gather her into his arms. As he reached out to touch her she swatted his hands away and knelt in front of him.

Wordlessly, she grasped his cock at the base and licked the underside of his shaft. She started at the bottom and worked her way to the head.

Then she repeated the movement over and over, licking him everywhere. His brain was barely functioning as she ran her tongue and lips over every inch of his cock.

With one hand he reached for the wall and used it for support. Oh yeah, this was definitely a dream. This couldn't be happening. It sure felt real enough though.

The running water of the shower pounded against his back but he was big enough that she was barely sprayed.

Not that she seemed to notice, she was so intent on what she was doing. Finally, she stopped teasing him and took his head fully in her mouth. He tried to bite it back, but a loud groan escaped as she lowered her lips over him.

As she worked his length, he closed his eyes and focused on the pleasure. What felt like tiny zings of electricity zapped down his spine and through his legs, all the way to his toes. He was so close to release, it bordered on painful.

She continued working him with her mouth and pumping him with her hand. The dual movements proved to be the perfect rhythm. When she lightly tugged on his sac, the unexpected sensation pushed him over the edge.

His balls pulled up tight and his hips jerked erratically. Before he could even think to warn her, he exploded. Long, hot streams of come hit the back of her throat but she didn't stop sucking him until she'd taken all he had to give.

Breathing heavily, he waited a moment before opening his eyes because he feared what he'd see. When he did, he let out a long sigh.

He wasn't in his shower, but in his big bed.

Alone.

Even though he'd been fairly sure it had all been a dream, his gut tightened. As if on cue, the buzzing of his alarm went off. Perfect freaking timing. How the hell was he going to work with Carly and keep his hands to himself after this?

Normally he ran in the evenings, but because of how he felt, he'd need another run this morning. Throwing off the covers, he opened the sliding glass door that led from his bedroom to the lanai.

He didn't bother covering himself as he stepped outside. His pack owned miles and miles of private beach in the Key Biscayne area. He wasn't worried about anyone but the seagulls seeing him naked. Many werewolves and shifters preferred the mountains, but after years of living in mountainous terrain all over the globe, his father—his Alpha—had decided to settle in Miami.

As long as they had a place to run free, the pack could live in peace. Changing was a part of who they were. If they weren't free to change on a regular basis, they'd have no control over themselves and would eventually go crazy or get sick and die.

The sun was just peeking over the horizon so shadows danced off palm trees and other foliage. As he glanced along the beach, his gaze narrowed when he saw a familiar dark wolf standing by one of the sand dunes.

Without pausing, Nick changed. The pain was inevitable. It would hit like lightning, then fade just as quickly, blending into something much more pleasurable. As his bones shifted and broke and realigned, he focused on the rush of rapture that surged over him once he was in animal form.

Bounding over to his brother, he knocked Stephan down in a playful gesture. *What are you doing out this early?* he projected with his mind.

Stephan jumped up and swatted at the sand with his paw, kicking up the grains. *I just got off a late shift and need to blow off some steam.*

Nick loved his brother but the last thing he wanted to do now was talk. *Think you can beat me to Aunt Caro's house?*

In response, Stephan leapt away from him and darted toward the harder, wet earth lining the beach.

Nick chose to run along the softer sand as he raced down the shore. It was harder on his muscles, but it kept him in shape. In wolf form, everything was intensified. The salty smell of the ocean, the crisp breeze, the sand underneath his paws. As his muscles strained, a much-needed calmness rolled over him. An extra run was exactly what he needed.

CHAPTER THREE

Carly glanced at herself in the rearview mirror of her car one more time before getting out. A wave of heat immediately greeted her. First day jitters hummed through her body as she walked toward the glass door. She couldn't believe she'd gotten a job so quickly. Interviewing at Nick's Auto Shop had been part of her plan to get used to interviews again. As a way to ease back into the job-hunting game.

For some reason she couldn't get rid of the queasy sensation in her gut. She'd never been nervous about a job before. If only her new boss didn't have that tall, dark, and sexy thing going on. Dark hair, pale gray eyes, bronzed skin, and incredible muscles. The sleeves of his mechanic coveralls had been rolled up yesterday, revealing corded arms and a couple interesting-looking tattoos. She usually dated lawyers, CPAs or other white-collar guys and while most of the men she'd been with were in decent shape, no one had ever compared to the hulking Nick Lazos.

31

Not that she should even be thinking about her boss in that capacity. She'd been so nervous in the interview yesterday she hadn't been able to stop herself from rambling. At least he hadn't seemed to notice. Hell, he hadn't seemed interested in one word she'd said. That was why she couldn't believe he'd even hired her.

Nervously she smoothed a hand down her wrap dress then inwardly gave herself a pep talk. She was really good at what she did. Working in an auto shop was something she'd never done before but numbers were numbers. Didn't matter where she worked. So even if he intimidated her, she knew what she was doing.

The little bell jingled above the door as she entered. To her surprise, Mr. Lazos—Nick—stood behind the main counter. She'd assumed since he was the owner he'd come in later.

Immediately butterflies took flight in her stomach as they made eye contact but she managed a smile. "Morning."

"Morning." He watched her with that pale gaze, as if he knew she was attracted to him.

Well thank God he couldn't actually read her mind. If he could, she'd be in serious trouble. As her thoughts strayed to what lay beneath his coveralls, she cursed having the complexion of a redhead. She could actually feel her cheeks heat up.

"Hot out there," he grunted.

"Yeah. Still getting used to this weather." She unhooked her purse from her shoulder as she walked around the counter.

"All your references had great things to say about you. Why'd you move to Miami anyway?"

"Needed a change of scenery and my grandmother lives here." She avoided his gaze as she brushed past him toward the small office. No way was she telling him all the details of why she'd left Chicago. "Should I just put my purse in here?"

He followed her in so that she had no choice but to lean against the desk.

"Yeah. Listen, my last assistant left without any notice. I've already turned on the computer for you and that stack over there is everyone's time cards. Payroll needs to be finished by Friday."

"That shouldn't be a problem. What program do you use?"

When he rattled off the name of an accounting program she was familiar with, she breathed an inward sigh of relief. She'd been expecting someone to train her, but it looked like she was going to be doing everything herself.

He continued. "From what I can tell everything looks in order, but if you have any questions, don't hesitate to grab me from the pit. In a few weeks I'll have you help out with the phones but for now, I've forwarded everything to the pit. I just want you focusing on payroll. My people need to get paid on time."

"Okay."

"Oh, you get an hour for lunch. Take it whenever you want, just let me or one of the guys know."

She nodded and he left before she could think if she had any questions. Okay then, looked like she really was on her own. She was thankful he wasn't a micromanager, but she was still a little nervous that he was trusting her with so much. Tucking a strand of hair behind her ear, she looped around the desk and sat.

At least the office wasn't as messy as yesterday. Once she'd gotten used to her job, she was definitely cleaning this place up. And maybe she'd hang up a couple of pictures. It wasn't that the room was dirty, just unorganized and bland.

As she pulled up the program and got to work, relief coursed through her as she started cross-checking the time cards and employees. It would be time-consuming to get caught up with everything, but for the most part, everything was preset.

Three hours later, she was massaging the back of her neck when a female voice caused her to glance up.

"You must be the new girl." A pretty brunette wearing one of the blue jumpsuits stepped into the office.

"Uh, yeah."

"I'm Alexandra but you can call me Alex."

Carly stood. "I'm Carly. I didn't know there were any female..." She stopped, realizing how sexist she sounded.

The other woman grinned. "I get that all the time but I grew up working on cars. I'm about to head to lunch. You want to come with me?"

"Sure." She grabbed her purse from under the desk and followed Alex out. Nick had said she could go to lunch when she wanted and she needed a mental break.

The petite woman opened the glass door that led to the pit and shouted that they were leaving to eat.

Once they were outside, Carly automatically walked toward her car but Alex stopped her and motioned across the street to a one-story Cuban restaurant. "Want to go to Molina's?"

"Sure." Even though she'd been in Miami a couple weeks, Carly hadn't had as much time to get used to the area as she'd hoped.

"So why'd you move to Miami?" Alex asked as they waited at the crosswalk.

"I wanted to be closer to my grandmother but I also needed a change of scenery."

"Because of a man?" Alex's teasing voice instantly put her at ease.

She shrugged and decided to be honest. "That was part of the reason."

"There are plenty of men here. Just don't date anyone at the shop. They're all pigs. Well, except Nick. He's my cousin though so I kind of have to say that." Alex stepped onto the road as the light changed.

"Trust me, I don't plan on dating anyone for a while." Getting settled into a new place and a new job was enough to take up her time without worrying about jumping back into the dating game.

"No, *trust me*, you'll change your mind once you see all the hot men on South Beach."

She couldn't disagree with her there. "I actually got to check out the beach last week."

"And?"

Carly bit back a grin. "Okay, you're right. There were a lot of good-looking men but I don't want to date a man who works out more than me."

Alex chuckled under her breath. "Stick with me and I'll introduce you to all the eligible men worth meeting. My brother's birthday is this Friday and we're having a big party at my parents' house if you want to come," she said as she opened the door to the restaurant.

Carly avoided answering as the hostess greeted them. Alex was really sweet but she also looked like she was barely twenty-one. Something told Carly she was still into partying and clubbing. Carly had definitely done her share of partying in college, but staying out until three in the morning didn't interest her anymore. Still, she couldn't help but wonder if Nick would be there.

* * *

Nick glanced up as Alex strolled back into the garage. He was bent over the open hood of a '65 Impala, but he pushed up. The other guys were still at lunch so he nodded her over. "Alex, got a sec?"

"What's going on?"

"How was your lunch?"

Her brow furrowed, probably because he'd never asked her before. "Fine."

Okay, so she wasn't going to make this easy and he couldn't make his attraction to Carly obvious. "Do you think Carly's going to work out?"

His cousin nodded. "I hope so. She's a little quiet but I really like her. Oh, I invited her to Phillip's party Friday."

Phillip's party? He frowned, trying to remember what the party was for. In their family, there was always a birthday or anniversary to go to. Considering most of the pack was at least a century old, it was a lot of events to remember.

"Don't tell me you forgot! It's his birthday."

"I didn't forget," he muttered.

"Yeah, right." She cleared her throat and glanced over her shoulder toward the office. "Boss, I know everyone else can't smell you but good Lord, tone it down. If you don't, even Carly's going to know you want to jump her bones."

Damn it. Alex was from a much younger generation and she was still learning to control the impressions she put off. The fact that she felt the need to remind *him*, told him he might have a problem. He thought he'd done a pretty good job of masking his lust, but apparently not. Hell, after the vivid, practically multicolored dream from last night, who the hell could blame him.

"Noted. Now get back to work, slacker." He grinned as she rolled her eyes.

Even though she was young and sometimes unpredictable, Alex was one of the best employees he had. Besides, she was his cousin. He wasn't sure how he felt about her hanging around with Carly though. Alex was too wild. Grabbing a rag, he wiped off his hands and headed inside.

He found Carly shutting one of the drawers of the desk. She didn't notice him at first and when she saw him, she gave a slight jump, the scent rolling off her a mix of surprise and... not exactly guilt, but close to it. Maybe embarrassment. It was too difficult to tell. "Hey," she said, her voice slightly trembling.

"Everything okay?"

"Yeah," she said a little too quickly. It was subtle and she probably wasn't aware of it but her gaze darted back to the drawer she'd just closed.

He wasn't even going to pretend he wasn't interested. He doubted she was stealing from him since there wasn't much for her to take in here, but he didn't like that scent. "What's in the drawer?"

Her cheeks flushed pink and to his annoyance, he found he liked that way too much. "I... Okay, I don't want you to think I was doing this during work hours, especially not on my first day. Or at all, even. I'd planned to use my lunch break, but then Alex asked me so... and now I'm rambling." She slid the door open to reveal a tote bag next to her purse.

She hadn't brought the bag in this morning so she must have grabbed it after lunch or sometime earlier.

"I pulled this out of my car because I didn't want it sitting out in the heat."

"What is it?" He could see rolled yarn and a long needle sticking out.

"Ah, it's my knitting bag. And yes, I know I have the hobby of an eighty year old lady and I don't care." Her cheeks were crimson now, her scent almost defensive.

He snickered, unable to stop himself. Well, hell, she wasn't stealing, she just knitted. He found that beyond adorable. "You were hiding your knitting?"

"I didn't want you to think I was slacking off."

"What do you knit?"

She blinked in surprise. "Oh, ah, well mainly just scarves, though I won't need them down here very often. Around the holidays I make these miniature little sweaters and use them as gift ornaments. They're insanely cute. And I've made throws, but only if I can find really fantastic wool... and I'm rambling again. You were just being polite." The blush was back.

The sight of her flustered did strange things to him. He'd never liked that whole innocent quality to a woman before, but damn it, he liked it on Carly. Way too much "No, I'm really interested. Maybe you can make me something." He wanted to take the words back as soon as he'd said them, but then she smiled and relaxed.

"Maybe I will." She glanced back at the computer, sending a lock of that silky red hair cascading over her shoulder. He wondered what it would feel like sliding between his fingers. "I've done a lot of reviewing so far today and the last accountant left everything in pretty good order."

"Good. Listen, when all the guys get back I'll introduce you to everyone." He couldn't believe he hadn't done it earlier, but he hadn't been thinking straight around her. Actually, he hadn't been thinking at all. At least not with his brain.

"Sounds good." Her words came out a little breathless, sending an alert straight to his cock.

Nope, he wasn't doing this, wasn't going to be attracted to her. He would simply fight his urges. He nearly snorted at the stupidity of his own thought. "I hear you're coming to my cousin's party Friday."

"Yeah. That was really sweet of Alex to invite me." Carly turned in her chair to face him.

"I'll probably see you there." What the hell was the matter with him? He shouldn't be hanging around her office making small talk. Every second that ticked by, his cock got harder.

At his words, a light shade of pink played across her cheeks. "Okay."

It wasn't overt, but a whiff of something akin to desire tickled his nose. He wished he knew what was going on in that pretty head of hers, but his brain froze, making any further conversation impossible. He grunted something and left her in peace. He'd never had a problem around women. Talking to women came as naturally as breathing. Of course he'd never been around a woman who made his tongue swell and his cock hard without any sort of stimulation. Just talking to her and he felt like a randy pup again with his first crush.

"Can you take a look at this, boss?" Jimmy asked as he walked across the garage.

Nick stopped by the Mercedes Jimmy was working on. "Yeah. What's up?"

"I can't figure out..."

Nick made the mistake of glancing toward the store. The garage and store were connected by glass doors and glass windows so he could see practically everything going on inside. His office was the only room he couldn't see, but Carly wasn't in there. He knew that because she was talking to one of his guys. Jimmy's words faded away as he watched Rodrigo, his newest hire, leaning against one of the counters talking to Carly.

Whatever he was saying must be fucking hilarious. Carly's red hair swished seductively around her shoulders as she clutched her stomach laughing. All he could think about was the fictional memory of watching her hair cascade around his cock while she sucked him. It made him want to walk inside and slam his fist across Rodrigo's face for simply talking to her.

Despite being raised in a shifter family where the alpha and beta lines were clearly drawn, he'd always considered himself fairly enlightened when it came to the opposite sex—shifter or human. He'd never before experienced such barbaric inclinations about any woman.

Rodrigo was lucky he was still breathing. Gritting his teeth, he tore his gaze away and inwardly groaned. What the hell had he been thinking by hiring her?

CHAPTER FOUR

Carly shut the computer down with a satisfied sigh. Her first day had flown by surprisingly fast. Alex had told her that most of the guys were pigs, but everyone she'd talked to had been so nice.

A lot nicer than where she'd worked in Chicago. Maybe it had something to do with the sunny weather, but practically everyone she'd come in contact with in Miami was friendly.

"You getting out of here?" Nick's deep voice cut through her thoughts.

God, how did he do that? The man was like a ghost. "Yeah. Unless you need me to stay…"

"No, we're shutting down too. Unless there's an emergency, I don't keep my guys past five."

She grabbed her purse from the drawer in her desk and fished her keys out. Nick was still standing by the door and she wondered if she was supposed to say something else. She'd noticed him looking at her a few times today and of course it had been when she was talking to one of the employees.

Maybe he thought she wasn't taking her job seriously. She frowned at the thought.

"So how was your first day?" His lips pulled up at the corners but she couldn't figure out if that was supposed to be his version of a smile. He was incredibly hard to read, but he didn't seem annoyed with her so that was good.

"It was great. I hope it's okay, but I made a couple changes with the way some of your billing is set up." She snapped her mouth shut because she could feel herself starting to ramble. *Again.* Since she'd already embarrassed herself with that little knitting revelation, she didn't need to add to it.

"I'd like to review any changes you make." His deep voice sent shivers to all her nerve endings.

She nodded and swallowed the lump in her throat. "I figured. I kept notes of everything I changed—which wasn't much," she added hastily.

"If you're ready, I'll walk you to your car." There was something positively sensual about the way he looked at her.

She was sure it wasn't intentional, but when he stared at her with those pale eyes, she wanted to do bad, bad things to him. And that wasn't like her at all. Carly normally dated a man for weeks, usually months before even contemplating sleeping with him. Nick Lazos only needed to look at her and she was ready to strip her clothes off and let him have his way with her. Ugh. He was her *boss*, she reminded herself for the hundredth time that day.

Somehow she ordered her legs to move. She needed to get out of there before she did or said something incredibly stupid. No need to embarrass herself in front of the sexy man.

The sweltering Florida heat wasn't as bad as it had been in the early afternoon, but her face and body warmed the instant they stepped outside. She'd parked directly out front so she wasn't exactly sure why he wanted to walk with her. Jangling her keys in her hand she smiled at him. "Well, thanks. I'll see you tomorrow."

He nodded, but to her dismay he waited while she got into her car. For the past week she'd been having trouble with her little two-door car. Her normally trusty car had gotten her through college and then some, but the drive to Florida had been pretty rough. She turned the ignition and held her breath when she turned the key. "Come on, baby, don't let me down now." Not in front of Nick.

This morning it had sputtered and sputtered until it finally started. This evening, it didn't even do that much for her. "Do not do this to me. Come on," she ordered through gritted teeth. She tried turning the key again but it simply made a clicking sound.

She had no choice but to turn when Nick knocked on her window. Taking a deep breath, she took the key out and opened the door. "My car's been giving me some trouble, but it's no big deal. My grandmother will pick me up so—"

"I'll give you a ride." He held out a big, callused hand.

Briefly she wondered what it would be like to feel that hand stroking over her bare skin. Just as quickly she felt her cheeks heat up. Oh yeah, she definitely didn't need to be in an enclosed space with her sexy as sin boss if that was the direction of her thoughts. "Oh, no—"

"If you give me your car key, I'll come back tonight and see if I can figure out what's wrong with it."

Carly clutched the keys in her hand. "That's okay. I couldn't ask you to do that."

"Carly. You work at an auto shop. Take advantage of the free labor." His words were low and somehow sensual, but they almost sounded like an order. Maybe that should rub her the wrong way, but she wouldn't mind him ordering her around. At least in the bedroom.

Something told her people rarely said no to him. Especially women. Averting her gaze, she slid the key off the ring and placed it in his outstretched palm. When her fingers brushed his, an electric current sent an unexpected shock straight to her core.

Her gaze flew to his and she almost stumbled at what she saw. Pure, raw lust flared in his eyes. It was only there for a split second but she knew what she'd seen.

Well, that was unexpected—and not exactly un-welcome. Clearing her throat, she found her voice. "If you're sure you don't mind taking me home, I'm ready."

"I definitely don't mind," he murmured, his tone sensual.

Oh hell. Her boss was interested in her. It was probably just a simple little attraction that would never amount to anything, but knowing a man that hot thought she was attractive did something crazy to her libido.

Carly knew what she looked like. She was cute in a girl-next-door kind of way, but men like Nick rarely looked twice at her. Maybe the men in Miami were different. Another score for the sunny city.

"Wait here, I'll pull my car around." He turned and had disappeared back inside the garage before she could blink.

Placing a hand on her abdomen, she took a few deep breaths. *Get it together*, she ordered herself. She was being ridiculous.

A few seconds later she heard Nick before she saw him. His two-door muscle car rumbled quietly as he drove around from the back of the building. She didn't know exactly what kind of car it was, but it was definitely hot. And it totally fit him.

He stopped a few feet from her and before she could move, he jumped out and opened the door for her.

Oh, this was bad. Very, very bad. He was sexy and chivalrous. "I live off La Salle Street," she said a few seconds later when he slid into the driver's seat.

"I know where that is." He didn't glance at her as he spoke.

She asked another question just to hear his voice. "How long have you lived in Miami?"

"I grew up here."

Okay, so maybe he didn't feel like making conversation. That normally wouldn't bother her. It was actually a pet peeve of hers when people felt the need to fill all silences. She clutched her purse in her lap as he turned down a side street.

The muscles in her arms and legs were incredibly tense. It was nice that he'd offered her a ride home, but it was also making her very aware that maybe her little crush was growing out of control. Which seemed insane on too many levels. She'd just met the man. "Do you mind if I turn on the radio?"

"Go ahead." There he went with that smooth voice again.

With the exception of the radio, the rest of the ride to her place was in silence, which was a little unnerving. When he started to pull into the driveway of the main house, she pointed to the extended drive along the side of the house.

"I live in the apartment back there." To her annoyance her voice had dropped a couple notches, taking on an almost sensual quality. Good Lord, she needed to get away from this man and fast.

"Do you need a ride in the morning?" he asked as he put his car in park.

"No, I'll be okay. I really appreciate you taking me home though. See you tomorrow." Holding her purse, she hurried out.

To her dismay, he opened his door and followed her up the short stone walk.

Nick raked a hand through his dark hair and cleared his throat. "Listen, Carly, I'm sorry if I've made you feel uncomfortable or anything."

She blinked. "Uncomfortable?"

"Shit. I can't think straight around you," he muttered.

"Wait, *what?*" Did he mean what she thought he did?

Those pale gray eyes of his locked with hers and her heart stuttered in her chest. He was only a few inches from her now. Their surroundings seemed to funnel out as they watched each other.

Before she realized what he intended, he cupped her cheek with his big hand. The feel of his callused palm against her skin sent a foreign flutter to her stomach. She could feel the vein in her neck pump as anticipation hummed through her.

What was he doing? Okay, she knew what he planned to do, could see it clearly in his eyes. Was she insane for letting him? Maybe so but it was hard to care. Nervously she licked her lips. The small motion tore his gaze away from hers as he zeroed in on her mouth.

Yep, she was right. He was going to kiss her. This had disaster written all over it, but that didn't stop her from wanting a taste of him.

Lips that had looked hard and unforgiving were surprisingly gentle as they covered hers. As soon as they made contact, her body molded against his. There were a dozen different reasons she knew this was the dumbest thing she'd ever done, but all she could focus on was the way he tasted.

Sweet and minty. Another surprise.

His tongue moved over hers in erotic little strokes. As if they had a will of their own, her hands wound their way around his neck.

The hand that had been cupping her cheek now clutched the back of her head in a tight, possessive grip. Moaning, she pressed her body against the full length of him, savoring the feel of her breasts against his muscular chest. Unfortunately there was a whole mess of clothes in their way. She wanted to feel his skin against hers. That thought should have brought her up short, but as she kissed him, she craved so much more.

A slow-moving heat slid down her belly and between her legs like hot lava. She'd never been so affected by anyone before. And she'd never been bowled over by one kiss either.

Heat and cream dampened her panties as he slowly trailed a hand down her back toward her backside. When he cupped her ass and squeezed, she moaned into his mouth.

This was crazy. They needed to get inside now before she let him take her up against her front door for anyone to see. Pulling her head back she kept her fingers linked around the back of his neck. Before she could say a word, however, he stepped away from her.

"Shit," he muttered and raked a hand through his hair. "I'm sorry...I'm..." His words trailed off as he turned on his heel and jogged toward his vehicle.

A tight knot formed in her stomach as he tore out of the driveway. What the hell had just happened? She'd been ready to throw herself at her boss. Her boss!

Groaning aloud, she opened her front door and locked the door tightly behind her. Part of her wanted to hide her head in the sand and not go into work tomorrow. Or ever. But she knew she couldn't do that. Finding a job so quickly had been a miracle. Not to mention the pay and the benefits were fantastic. Besides, he was the one who'd kissed her. If he had a problem, then too bad. He could just deal with it.

CHAPTER FIVE

Three Days Later

Nick steered his 1968 Dodge Charger into his Aunt Melina's long driveway. Unlike most of the pack, his aunt preferred living closer to the city limits of Miami instead of in Key Biscayne. There were almost a dozen cars already lining the street and three currently in the driveway. He didn't see Carly's car, but Alex had told him she was picking up the redheaded vixen he couldn't get out of his head so he knew she was already here.

For the past three days he'd been able to avoid her. There had been a few awkward moments, but he'd mastered his Houdini act. Kissing her had been the dumbest move he could have made. He wanted to talk to her about it and apologize, but he was afraid if he tried to talk to her, he'd kiss her again. Not to mention, he wasn't sorry and he doubted he could fake it.

A bang on his window made him turn to find his younger brother, Stephan, standing there. He inwardly cursed his lack of awareness. For the past week all his senses had been off kilter. He should have smelled Stephan. Instead all his energy and thoughts were focused on Carly.

Immediately he opened the door. "Hey, surprised to see you here. Tell me I'm not the last one."

"Just about." Stephan slapped him on the back and pulled him into a tight hug.

"Are you working a case right now?" Nick locked his car before shutting the door.

"Nah. Just came off one. Thought I'd see the family before I got reassigned." His brother raked a hand through his dark hair.

"You need a haircut." He shook his head as they walked up the steps. Stephan had been working for the Drug Enforcement Administration for the past four years.

"Tell me about it... Hey, who's the hot redhead human Alex brought? She smells like sex and—"

"She's off limits. To you, to anyone. She's *mine*," Nick growled. The second the words were out of his mouth, he knew it was true. It was the only thing that made sense. Carly *was* his. He'd stopped looking for a mate a long time ago. And he'd never thought his mate would be a human. But it was the only thing that explained his intense attraction to her.

"Oh, shit. Never thought I'd see the day. You actually think she's your mate? A human?" Stephan asked as they reached the front door of his aunt's two-story Mediterranean-style house.

"Just stay away from her," he bit out. It was a struggle to simply keep his wolf in check right now.

"Hmm, if you haven't claimed her, she's fair game." Stephan's voice was taunting as he opened the front door.

The only thing keeping Nick from actually punching his brother was that he knew Stephan was just fucking with him. "I'd hate to kick your ass if—"

The second they stepped onto the tiled foyer, his Aunt Melina grabbed both their arms. For such a small female, she had a wicked grip. "Stephanos, where did you sneak off to? Nicolas, you're *late*! And where's Thomas?"

"I think he's working, but Stephan wanted to ask you about that salon you go to. He needs a haircut." Nick dropped a quick kiss on her cheek and headed down the long hallway toward the kitchen. He threw a glance over his shoulder and gave his scowling brother the finger.

If he allowed her, his aunt would hold his ear captive for half an hour. And he had more important things to worry about. Like finding Carly.

In the kitchen he found three of his younger female cousins whispering around the table. When they saw him they all giggled.

"What's so funny?" He looked back and forth between them.

Athena, one of his favorites, answered. "Nothing much. Alex just told us a story about you when you were our age."

He frowned. Athena wasn't more than fifteen or sixteen. She was barely a pup. When she turned twenty, her aging process would slow down immensely, allowing her to live hundreds of years. Hell, maybe longer. It wasn't as if it was an exact science.

He remembered quite well what he'd been like back then. It had been over a century ago and he'd been living in Greece.

Sighing, he thought of his hometown of Leontio. Being a shifter had been a lot easier back then. Greeks in general had a lot of respect for wolves and mythology and the thought of the paranormal wasn't scoffed at as it was in so many other places around the globe. "Where exactly is Alex?" he asked through gritted teeth.

With a big, knowing grin plastered on her face, Athena nodded toward the back of the house. "Back porch. Hey, where's Thomas? I haven't seen him in like, a month, and he promised to help me with a school project on the history of Greece."

"He's working," he answered absently as he opened the back door.

Wherever Alex was, Carly was sure to be also. As he stepped onto the back porch, he swept his gaze around the throng of people. There were about twenty-five of his relatives and friends of friends, shifters and humans alike, eating and drinking. A few sat in lounge chairs around the Olympic-sized pool, some stood in clusters, and one of his uncles and two male cousins stood around the grill arguing about a football game. His Uncle Cosmo had remarried a few decades ago and now his pack had a new generation of werewolves who were more in touch with their human side. They'd all grown up in the city and while they understood their heritage and their order in the pack, they didn't seem to take things as seriously as his generation.

Nick mentally shook himself as he zeroed in on Carly. Even if he hadn't been able to smell her sweet scent, she was the easiest to spot. In a sea of dark-haired men and women, her red hair and fair skin was like a beacon.

Unwanted jealousy jolted through him, sharp and deadly, when he spotted her talking to a man he didn't recognize. She held a glass of white wine in one of her slim hands and was smiling politely while that randy bastard practically undressed her with his eyes.

Fuck that.

If she was his mate, he needed to clear the air with Carly if he was ever going to get a decent night's sleep again. Not to mention he owed her a big apology.

In a few long strides he stood in front of Carly and the man.

"Carly." Her name rolled off his tongue with ease. For the past couple nights he'd fantasized about saying her name as that long hair fanned against his chest while she rode him.

Her pretty blue eyes widened as she shifted to face him. "Oh hi, Nick." When she bit her bottom lip in that adorable way he was coming to love, he bit back a groan. He wanted to be the one biting that lip.

"I'm Dennis." The other man nodded at him politely, but he couldn't mask the wave of annoyance that rolled off him.

Nick stared at the man for a moment. His green eyes had a strange quality, but Nick couldn't place him. The guy smelled human, but there was something else there too. Something earthy and slightly familiar? Nick inwardly cursed himself. He was sizing this guy up just because he was talking to his woman. He didn't give a shit what the guy smelled like. "Nice to meet you," he said through clenched teeth. "Hope you don't mind if I steal Carly for a second. Shop talk."

Nick didn't wait for a response as he hooked his hand under Carly's elbow and steered her toward two lone chairs by the pool.

"What are you doing?" she muttered.

"Do you want to sit?" He motioned to the lounge chair.

"Fine." She sat and when she crossed those long legs, his cock jumped to attention.

Following suit, he sat next to her. She wore white shorts that showcased her sinfully long legs and a turquoise halter top that showed off her graceful neck. The thought of raking his teeth over that delicate skin caused another unwanted reaction.

"How's your car running?" It had taken him about an hour Tuesday night to figure out what was wrong, but it had been an easy fix. He'd even changed her oil.

"Better than before, actually, thank you. Do you really want to talk about my car?" she asked quietly.

He cleared his throat and forced himself to maintain eye contact. "We haven't had a chance to talk since...ah..." He cleared his throat again. Damn, it shouldn't be this hard to talk to her.

"Since you kissed me." Her words were tight and restrained.

"Right."

"And whose fault is that? You've been ignoring me all week," she snapped. The unexpected fire in her eyes and the heat in her voice made him change tactics.

He hadn't realized just how feisty Carly was. "You're right. I should have talked to you sooner. I've never behaved like that with an employee and I owe you an apology. Hell, I owe you more than that. If you want to file a sexual harassment charge against me, you have more than enough right to. I won't fight you." Werewolf or not, he was a man first and he'd had no right to treat Carly the way he had. Even if Carly had returned the kiss, he was her boss and he'd put her in an awkward position.

She watched him carefully, her expression far too neutral. "Did you enjoy the kiss?"

Did she even have to ask? "It's all I've thought about the past three days."

A smiled teased her very kissable mouth. "Me too... I don't want to file a harassment charge against you, Nick. Trust me."

"Then what do you want?"

"You." Her lips parted a fraction, as if she'd surprised herself with the admission. "Damn, I shouldn't have had that second glass," she murmured as she placed her near-empty wineglass next to her chair.

Shit, the woman was sending all his good intentions out the window. The twinge of lust he'd smelled a few days ago was now full blown. The spicy scent rolled over him with an unexpected intensity. He'd been walking around with a permanent hard-on the past few days and feeling doubly guilty for practically mauling his new employee on her first day. And she still wanted him? "Do you want to get out of here?" he rasped out.

Her eyes widened for a split second, but she simply nodded.

"Good. I'll tell Alex you're not feeling well and that I'm taking you home." He glanced over his shoulder. No one was paying attention to them. "Head through the house and I'll meet you out front in a few minutes."

Her cheeks had turned pink, but she nodded and stood on shaky legs.

He waited in his seat for a minute longer to compose himself. Once he'd managed to get his thoughts and body under control, he found his cousin, gave her a quick excuse, then managed to avoid talking to anyone as he escaped out the front door. He knew Alex hadn't believed him and considering the lusty vibe he knew he was putting off, Nick guessed every shifter in the house knew *exactly* why he was leaving.

He didn't give a shit.

Nick found Carly leaning against his car and his breath caught in his throat. All he could envision was her stretched out on his hood wearing nothing but a pair of heels.

"Do you want to grab a bite to eat or hit up some of the clubs? My older brother owns one on South Beach." Somehow he managed to string multiple coherent sentences together. She might have said she wanted to leave, but she didn't say she wanted to head back to his place and fuck for hours. That was what *he* wanted to do.

She glanced down at herself then back up at him. "If we go downtown I'll need to change first."

He bit back his disappointment. "No problem." He hated the Miami nightlife and if it wasn't for the fact that his brother owned a club, he'd never go in the first place. He might have offered to take her out, but all he really wanted to do was get her back to his place and flat on her back. Or against a wall. Or bent over the side of his bed. Or hell, right on his car. He'd take her wherever and whenever she let him.

After opening the door for her he rounded the car and slid into the driver's seat.

"Was one of your brothers here earlier?"

He glanced in the rearview mirror before backing out. "Yeah, why?"

"I did a double take when I saw him. I thought it was you until he turned around."

He understood what she meant. They all had similar builds but both Nick's brothers had dark eyes. "That was Stephan. He's two years younger than me. Thomas is my older brother. He's the one who owns the club downtown."

"So it's just the three of you?" Out of the corner of his eye, he watched her shift in her seat and cross her legs toward him.

He forced himself to keep his gaze on the road and *not* her legs. Hard to do when all he could seem to think about was what it would be like to have those legs tossed over his shoulders as he tasted her. "Yep." Making any sort of conversation was damn near impossible. Nick racked his brain, trying to think of anything nonsexual to talk about. "Do you like Miami so far?"

Her face lit up instantly. "I love it here. The summers in Chicago are hot too so I'm looking forward to spending a fall here with no snow."

There, that wasn't so bad. He could talk like a normal human being. "What about the shop? I know we didn't get a chance to talk much this week, but are you figuring everything out okay?"

"Yeah. Most of the accounting stuff is time consuming since everyone has such different hours, but the programs you've got are great. And everyone has been really nice too, especially Alex."

He grunted at his cousin's name.

"What?"

"Nothing. She's just a pain in the ass sometimes. Needs a man to take care of her."

Carly's nose crinkled as she laughed aloud. The sweet sound enveloped him. "I can't believe you just said that. That's so chauvinistic."

He shrugged and glanced over his shoulder before switching lanes. Chauvinistic or not, it was true. For the next fifteen minutes he managed to talk to her like a normal person. That was a feat in itself.

Once they reached her place she invited him in while she got changed. Her apartment was small but from what he could see, it fit her. Large black-and-white prints of various American cities hung on two of the sage-colored walls. Bright afghan blankets were thrown across the back of the loveseat and couch and a vase of fresh sunflowers stood proudly on the coffee table. He wondered if she'd knitted the throws. If so, she was talented.

Carly's scent and movements caused him to look up from the magazine he'd grabbed off the coffee table. She was standing in the entryway of the hallway. He hadn't been actually reading, just staring at the pages and thinking of her. Everything inside him stilled at the sight of her. She wore a slim fitted two-toned purple and white dress with strappy heels. The cut was high, boat-neck, he thought maybe it was called, with some sort of lace overlay over the entire thing. "What do you think?" She turned once, her grin light and flirty.

It didn't show any cleavage but it was too short and too tight. And the back had a cut out, exposing way too much of her delectable skin. In reality it was perfectly respectable, tame even, compared to what most women wore to South Beach clubs, but he didn't want anyone else seeing all that toned skin. It was totally barbaric but he wanted her all for himself. His ancestors would be proud. Nick stood and forced himself to smile. "Hot."

She let out a short laugh. "That's certainly descriptive."

"You look beautiful," he amended. Hot wasn't the right description for her, even if she was exactly that. The woman was stunning and sweet—and all he could seem to think about was getting her naked.

There went the sexy blush. "Thanks," she murmured. "I'm ready if you are."

The living room was attached to a small foyer so he followed after her. As she started to unlock the front door, he instinctively placed his hand on the small of her back. Something primal inside him simply wanted to touch her, to claim her.

When he did, she looked back at him in surprise. White-hot lust flared in her eyes and the sweet scent of her desire washed over him like a tidal wave. In that instant, he knew they weren't going anywhere.

Her fiery red hair tumbled around her shoulders in seductive waves. Just like in his dream, only the reality was so much better. With a shaking hand, he threaded his fingers through her hair and cupped the back of her head. The desire to completely dominate her surprised him. He'd heard about what happened when other werewolves found their mates, but he'd never completely understood until now. And he really didn't want to fuck this up. Having a human mate wasn't something he'd counted on. If she'd been a shifter, she'd have recognized their connection and would have understood exactly what he needed from her.

"Do you want to stay or leave?" he rasped out.

Her tongue darted out to moisten her pink lips. "Stay," she whispered.

That was all he needed to hear. The second his mouth crushed over hers, he knew that everything he'd previously thought about women and relationships was about to change.

Drastically.

Nick knew Carly deserved wining, dining, and a lot of foreplay, but that would come later. Once he'd gotten his fill of her. Hell, if that was even possible.

He hadn't had a thing to drink, yet he felt almost drunk. Needing to feel more of Carly, he slid his free hand up her leg and under her sexy, lacy dress. His cock surged when he touched more bare skin than material. As he caressed and gripped her ass, she pressed her pelvis tightly against his and started grinding in small little circles.

The feel of her moving against him like that made him crazy.

Nick tore his mouth away from hers and feathered kisses along her jaw. Animalistic urges compelled him to kiss, touch, and claim every part of her body. He continued a trail down to her neck, savoring her sweet taste. A heady scent that was pure Carly enveloped and overwhelmed him, threatening to short circuit what few brain cells he had left.

He might have thought he'd had a clue what this would be like, but his erotic dream paled in comparison to the reality of actually touching her.

CHAPTER SIX

Carly couldn't believe what she was doing. This was her boss. Her very sexy boss, but still, this wasn't the smartest move she'd ever made. It was hard to care when he was touching her, when his hands were gently moving over her bare skin. Hell, it was hard to *think* straight when they were in the same room.

"Nick." His name rolled off her tongue when he pressed her back into the wall.

Every part of her ached with pent-up need. She'd been doing what was expected of her for too long. After her parents died, she'd been such a straight arrow, needing control over her life. It was part of the reason she'd gone into accounting. Numbers could never disappoint her.

Having sex with her boss would definitely qualify as poor decision making, yet she'd never wanted anything more, and she was going to take him.

As his hand glided over her bare skin and tugged at her thong, a shiver skittered through her, surging to all her nerve endings.

"You're so soft," he murmured against her neck.

His hand slid under the elastic of her panties and trailed around her hip until he reached her mound. Pushing the flimsy garment to the side, he gently rubbed a finger over her clit.

The unexpected touch made her jerk against him. She wanted so much more.

As he teased the sensitive bud, he slid his hands up her back and unsnapped the one button holding the keyhole of her dress up in the back. It easily slid down, only to pool around her waist. When she'd said she wanted to stay, she'd known what it meant for them, but being bared to him like this was still unnerving. Nick was such a huge, sexy guy. Sex appeal clung to him like some guys wore suits. It was simply part of his genetic makeup. She knew she was pretty, but it wasn't in that exotic, traffic-stopping way. She couldn't help but wonder if he would be disappointed once he saw all of her.

Nick completely stilled when her breasts were bared. His hand stopped moving over her slick folds and his eyes zeroed in on her chest.

She could feel her face heat up as a sudden wave of shyness overwhelmed her. She was tall and slim, but her breasts weren't much to look at. Instinct took over and she started to cover herself.

Nick grabbed both her wrists and pinned them to the wall above her head. The sudden abrupt action stole the breath from her.

"Don't ever cover yourself in front of me. You're fucking beautiful." His words were a low growl and somehow almost animalistic.

Something she found incredibly hot. She nodded since she didn't trust her voice. Still holding her arms in place, he dipped his head and sucked one of her nipples into his mouth. She moaned at the sharp, erotic action. Arching her back, she tried to give him better access, wanting so much more. Being pinned in place like this shouldn't be so arousing, but she grew damper each second that passed.

With each stroke and lick, an invisible ribbon of desire traveled straight to the throbbing between her legs. Her clit pulsed, aching for him to touch her there again. Pushing her hips forward deliberately, she lifted one of her legs and hooked it around his waist. She wasn't sure if this was a one-time thing and she planned to enjoy every second of their time together.

"Upstairs," she whispered in his ear, feeling a little bolder at his reaction to her. All the rooms in her place were downstairs except her bedroom, which took up the entire second floor.

Thankfully he understood what she meant—as if there could have been a doubt. His pale eyes flared when they met hers. As he dropped her arms, she instinctively linked her fingers together behind his neck. Before she could contemplate the ramifications of what they were about to do, he'd hoisted her up so she had no choice but to wrap her legs around him. He took the stairs two at a time, moving like a man possessed. Standing at five foot eight inches, she wasn't heavy but she wasn't a small woman either. Yet he moved with a grace and strength that surprised her.

As they entered her room she was aware of her feet touching the ground, but when the backs of her knees hit the end of her queen-sized bed, reality crashed down on her. They were moving really fast. Not that she didn't want this, she did. Way too much in fact. But, he was still her boss. "Do you think—"

"No thinking," he murmured before he clasped the bottom of her dress and pulled it over her head.

If she'd felt exposed before, it was nothing compared to standing in front of Nick in a skimpy thong and heels. She could feel her skin warm and her nipples harden as his pale gaze swept over her body. His chest lifted and rose erratically as he watched her.

Carly stood frozen, captured under his spell until it registered that he was still dressed. If she was going to be naked, so was he. She'd been fantasizing about him all week and wanted to see if the reality lived up to what she'd created in her mind.

Grasping his belt buckle, she tangled with it until it came free. As she pulled on the zipper, he lifted his shirt over his head and it was her turn to lose her breath.

She was vaguely aware that he'd kicked his pants out of the way but all she could focus on was his broad, oh-so-muscular chest. A man didn't have the right to look so good.

Dark hair lightly smattered across his pecs. The sharp lines across his chest and down his arms were perfectly defined and cut, as if he'd been chiseled from stone. He was like an incredibly honed machine. Everything about him was solid and sexy.

As her gaze strayed down his ripped abs to the V between his legs her face instantly warmed. His cock was long, thick and so perfect, her mouth actually watered. *Holy hell.* Soon he was going to be inside her. Her inner walls tightened at that thought.

"See something you like?" The deep timbre of his voice jerked her head back up to meet his gaze.

Before she could respond, he came at her fast, his mouth descending on hers with a ferocious, animalistic need.

Instinctively she braced herself for the fall as they tumbled onto the bed but Nick caught her around the waist and gently laid her against the comforter before settling his body against the full length of hers.

This was what she'd been waiting for. Skin on skin. Wrapping her legs around him, she rolled her hips against his. She felt frantic with the need to feel him inside her. After seeing how truly beautiful his thick length was, she wanted to feel every inch of it thrusting into her. Unfortunately he seemed content to take his time kissing her. The way his tongue swirled and danced in her mouth drove her senses haywire.

She'd always been big into foreplay but her body was so hot she felt as if she'd combust at any second. Getting Nick inside her was the only thing that seemed to matter.

When she reached between them and grasped his cock, his huge body stilled and he lifted his head back. His eyes flared with white-hot lust, a mirror of how she felt. "Did I say you could touch that?" he murmured.

A small smile touched her lips at the hint of dominance in his voice. "Do you want me to stop?"

"No, but I don't want to come in your hand." His voice rolled over her like honey as he bent and nipped her jaw.

The small admission told her he was just as turned-on as she was. Her fingers were still wrapped snugly around his cock, but she let go and both her hands trailed around to his backside.

If she couldn't touch that, then she was going to get her feel of the rest of his body. She dug her fingers into his ass and moaned as he continued kissing down her neck and chest. His hot breath on her skin sent tingles scattering over her entire body. She couldn't understand what it was about him that got her so crazy. Normally she had to date a man for a while until she was comfortable enough to take it to the next level. All Nick had to do was look at her and her clothes wanted to fall off.

He left a hot trail of kisses down her body until he reached her breasts. He licked and laved the underside of both, as if he was taking great care to cover every inch of her skin.

He lightly raked his teeth over one of her hardened nipples and began circling it in erotic little circles.

"Nick," she moaned out his name, needing more.

As if he read her mind, he pinched the other nipple between his forefinger and thumb and squeezed. The action bordered on pain, but sent shock waves straight to her pulsing core. Threading her fingers through his thick hair, she clutched onto his head as his tongue and fingers worked their torturous magic.

Her panties were completely soaked, something he had to know. "I want you inside me, now." Somehow she found the strength to utter a few coherent words.

Wordlessly he lifted up and tugged her panties down her hips and legs. She kicked one of her legs, sending the material flying off the bed.

Nick rubbed his thumb over her clit as he inserted one finger past her folds. He pulled it out then gently pushed two inside her. The sensation of him filling her, made another moan tear from her. When he pressed his fingers against her inner walls and slowly dragged them out, she nearly vaulted off the bed.

"You're so wet," he murmured as he withdrew his fingers and nestled between her thighs.

"Condom," she blurted as reality crashed over her. She might want him more than she'd wanted anyone, but they needed protection.

He paused, hovering at her entrance.

Nick inwardly cursed himself. It had been so long since he'd had sex with a woman who wasn't a shifter, he'd completely forgotten about condoms. Shifters didn't need protection because their DNA was completely different. He couldn't get STDs, which meant he couldn't give them. Not to mention female shifters could only get pregnant twice a year. But, Carly wasn't a shifter and she didn't know any of that. He could only hope she didn't think he was an irresponsible jackass.

"One sec." He slid off the bed and grabbed his wallet from the back of his pants. If his emergency condom wasn't in it, he didn't know what he'd do. When his fingers touched the foil packet, all his muscles tightened in anticipation.

His hands trembled as he sheathed himself and he cursed again. Carly was so receptive to his every touch, yet he still worried he'd somehow fuck this up and lose his mate.

By human standards he looked to be around thirty-two, give or take a couple years. In reality, he was almost one hundred and seventy. Losing her because of something so stupid wasn't an option. Never finding a mate was something he'd learned to accept. Or he thought he had. Now that he'd found Carly, he couldn't lose her because he was an idiot.

Gazing down at her, his breath caught. She stared at him with those big blue eyes, making it damn near impossible to breathe. He could drown in that gaze if he let himself.

"Are you ready?" he rasped out.

"Yes." The word fell from her lips without pause. Her eyes slightly dilated, her desire for him sharp.

After settling between her legs again, he pushed the head of his cock against her opening, wanting to give her time to adjust to his size. Even though he was bigger than most, he'd never had a problem in the past since most of his partners had been shifters. She might be taller than a lot of women, but everything about Carly was slim and delicate. And that included her sweet pussy.

Her inner walls clamped around him the farther he pushed. Oh, God, she was so damn tight.

"Am I hurting you?" he whispered.

She shifted her hips, thrust up and completely impaled herself on him with a harsh inhalation of breath. Then she locked her ankles around his waist and held firm. "I'm not going to break, Nick."

His throat was clenched too tight to talk. He stayed deeply buried inside her, savoring the feel of her clenching around his cock. If he moved, even a few inches, he knew he'd come and that wasn't acceptable.

Maybe it was a little superstitious, but he didn't care. When male werewolves mated, it was considered extremely bad luck if their mates didn't climax the first time. He'd been waiting more than a century to find her. He'd be damned if she didn't get off—more than once. Hell, whether it was bad luck of not, he wanted to see that ecstasy playing off her face as she came around his cock.

He cupped both her breasts and rubbed his thumbs over her pale pink nipples. When she let out a breathless sigh and her pussy clenched even harder around him, he knew he was headed in the right direction.

"Touch yourself," he ordered.

Her eyes flashed with brief surprise before she reached between her legs and began massaging her clit. Her lips parted seductively as she watched him.

The flush along her cheeks deepened as she continued stroking.

"*Fuck*, Carly." Watching her touch herself was one of the sexiest things he'd ever seen.

Leaning down, he kissed one of her breasts, taking care to lick and kiss all of the soft flesh. When she let out a tiny moan, he took a nipple between his teeth and sucked. Hard.

And that was all it took to push her over the edge.

"Oh!" She cried out, her hands going to his shoulders as she began rolling her hips against his in a frenzy.

Growling, he met her stroke for stroke. He grabbed her hips and searched out her mouth again. Hungrily he tasted her as he started moving in a rhythmic motion. He'd wanted their first time to last a lot longer but it simply wasn't going to happen.

He could smell her dampness and heat as she rode through her orgasm. It felt like a waterfall rushing over his cock as she came. He'd never experienced anything like it.

The combination of her sweet smell and tight body was all Nick needed. He tried to restrain himself but his climax rocketed through him with a roar. Clutching the sheets instead of her hips, he pounded into her. He was afraid of bruising her, even though the caveman part of him wanted her to have his marks on her hips, on her body. He wanted the whole damn world to know this female was his.

Groaning, he emptied himself in long, hard strokes. As he rode through the last wave, he pulled out and collapsed next to her, even if he could have stayed inside her all night.

"Holy shit," she muttered after a few long moments of silence.

"You can say that again."

"Say what again?" Still breathless, Carly propped up on one elbow and stared at him with a confused expression on her pretty face.

Oh shit. He'd heard of mates linking in various ways, but each couple reacted differently. His own parents could communicate telepathically but he'd never expected to experience the same thing. And definitely not with a human. Not to mention they hadn't officially bonded. He still needed to mark her and there was so much he needed to tell her. A healthy dose of worry slid through him at that thought, but he shelved it for now.

He rolled on his side and met her intense blue gaze. Feeling insanely possessive, he clutched onto her hip, needing to feel her soft skin again. He tightened his fingers against her. *Mine*, his wolf said. "I was just talking to myself, sweetheart."

A grin touched her face. *You can talk to yourself all you want as long as we do that again.*

No doubt about it now. She was definitely his mate. He fell back against the pillow and pulled her with him so that her head rested on his chest. Though he hated to do it, he put up a mental shield and forced himself to block out her thoughts. Until she realized what he was and what kind of connection they had, he couldn't invade her privacy. If she found out later that he had, he feared she'd hold it against him. Not to mention, if he could read her, then it was highly probable she could read him. If she didn't realize what was going on, she might think she was going crazy and that was the last thing he wanted.

Sighing, he hugged her tighter against him and inhaled her sweet scent. He loved the way she fit so perfectly against him. "Tell me more about yourself," he murmured after a few minutes.

She let out a sweet, amused laugh and dropped a kiss on his chest, though she didn't move more than that, just stayed curled up against him. "You don't exactly strike me as the kind of guy who likes to talk after sex."

He wasn't, but he wanted to know every damn thing about her. "Indulge me. So far I know you like to knit and that you look good in purple." Hell, she looked good in anything.

"Well that's good because it's my favorite color... All right, what do you want to know?"

"Do you have more family?"

"Ah, sort of. My parents died when I was fifteen. Car accident." He tightened his grip on her, wanting to offer comfort, but she rushed on. "My Grandma Kendall was my guardian. She was great, taking on a depressed teenager. She moved in to my parents' house so I wouldn't have to move anywhere new and was two parents rolled into one. My mom's parents didn't even come to their funeral. I'd never really thought about it until I lost them..." She let out a short, semi-bitter laugh.

"Why would I because I was a freaking teenager. Anyway, I'd never really thought about my mom being estranged from her parents. She never really came out and said it, but I guess nothing was ever good enough for them. I didn't comprehend what assholes they were until they simply didn't show up for their own daughter's funeral."

"I'm sorry, sweetheart." He rubbed a gentle hand down her spine, hating the pain he could feel rolling off her. The scent of it filled his nostrils, made his wolf edgy.

"It's okay. Well now it is. They mean nothing to me at this point. My grandma helped me through that really hard time and when I graduated high school I got as many scholarships as I could. I stayed living at home to save money and got the degree I wanted. Pretty boring," she murmured.

Not to him. "Is your grandma your only family then?"

"Yeah. When she moved here it was harder than I realized being separated from her. I think she'd planned to move to Florida earlier but then when my parents died, she really stepped up. God, I'm so lucky to have her. I know how differently things could have turned out if I hadn't."

"She's really sweet," he murmured.

"Right, I forgot you've met her. I still haven't met your mom. They play bunco or something together I think."

Nick nearly snorted. His mom was century's old but looked to be in her forties. Still, she preferred spending her time with older generations. "Yeah, my mom adores her."

"So what about you? I didn't realize everyone at that party was related. That's a whole lot of relatives."

Now he did snort. "No kidding. I'm not complaining though. And not everyone was related—just most of us. It could be that sex with you has fried my brain, but I can't even remember how many cousins I have right now."

She laughed against his chest. The sound soothed both the man and wolf. "Your family is loud and fun."

"Loud is an understatement," he murmured, kissing the top of her head. "So how'd you end up with a degree in business?" Considering she knitted she clearly had a creative side.

"I love numbers, always have. No matter what, they don't lie and they don't change." She sat up then and moved until she straddled him, taking him off guard.

The sight of her long, lean body on his had his cock lengthening again. Unfortunately he didn't have any more condoms—but he'd be remedying that soon. She trailed her fingers up his chest, as if she couldn't get enough of touching him.

"You like stability?"

She paused, contemplating her answer. "Yeah, I guess I do. It's probably not very sexy to admit, but—" She let out a little yelp as he moved lightning quick, flipping her so that she was underneath him.

"Everything you do is sexy, Carly," he murmured before capturing her mouth once again. He never wanted her to forget that.

CHAPTER SEVEN

Asha cursed as he pulled down the long circular driveway to his villa. He'd tried tracking the sexy redhead from the party, but he'd lost her scent. That was the problem with living in populated areas. All the smells and noises meshed together. It wasn't as if his extrasensory abilities were as strong as those of a werewolf or other shifters.

It had been sheer luck—or maybe fate—that he'd been invited to a party full of werewolves. And then to meet a woman who was an almost identical version of his first slave? Yes, it had to be fate. Of course the redhead wasn't a shifter, which was almost a pity. He hadn't fucked a lycan in nearly a century.

Thankfully, the partygoers hadn't realized he was Immortal. With the common, fake name of Dennis he'd given them, and the cloaking spell he'd cast, they had no reason to suspect what he was. The spell had been fading near the end, but it had lasted long enough for him to get out of there. Originally he'd gone to the party simply to check out the shifters living in Miami. It had been years since he'd visited the sunny city and last time he hadn't come across any nonhumans.

He placed his hand on the biometric scanner and entered the front door. The house was quiet, just as he'd left it.

"Slave," he bellowed.

Seconds later, the blonde with sharp, exotic cheekbones, that he'd recently acquired, descended the spiral staircase wearing a t-shirt that fell to mid-thigh. She came to stand before him, eyes downcast. A light bruise marred her left cheek.

He fingered the hem of the shirt. "What are you wearing, slave?"

Her head snapped up to meet his gaze. The terror and fear he saw in her blue eyes caused his cock to stir. He loved it when she begged for mercy.

"Don't make me ask again."

"You were gone. I thought...I thought it would be okay." She tucked a strand of hair behind her ear.

"You don't think, whore. You do as you're told." Asha held out his hand and watched her expression as a ball of fire formed in his extended palm.

The orange light reflected in her eyes as she stared at him. "What are you doing?" she whispered.

"I told you what would happen if you disobeyed me. I'll burn that pretty body of yours until you're unrecognizable. Then, I'll let you go."

She took a step back, tears streaming down her face. "I'm sorry. It won't happen again. I promise." Her voice and skinny body shook uncontrollably.

With his other hand he reached out and cupped the back of her skull in a tight, demanding grip. "Since you're new, I'll let it go. *This time.* Now, I'm going to make a drink. When I come upstairs, I want you at the foot of my bed on all fours, wearing nothing."

With wide eyes, she backed away from him and sprinted up the stairs.

Sighing, he headed to his study. Breaking in a new slave was always tedious. Sometimes he hated the twenty-first century. Back when he'd been a prince in Persia, his slaves had never questioned him and never back talked. They did what they were told because it was what they'd been bred to do. Mindless whores. That was all they were.

Which was why he came to Miami every few years. Normally he was able to buy quiet, malleable slave girls from the Russians, but the most recent one he'd gotten cried all the time. For a while she'd tried to insist she had a name. It was nauseating.

Something told him the redhead wouldn't come easily either. She wouldn't be a crier though, she'd probably fight him. He rubbed a hand over his crotch as he imagined her naked and tied to his bed. It had been a while since he'd had a woman with any spirit.

Tracking her down wouldn't be too hard. He already knew her friends. Before he left Miami, he was going to claim her. If she turned out to be as good as he imagined, he might even take her with him when he left for Dubai.

* * *

Carly opened her eyes, stretched her arms above her head and let out a big yawn. Oh yeah, she wouldn't mind staying in bed for another hour. But only if Nick spent it with her. Where was he anyway... She rolled over at the sound of her cell phone ringing. Plucking it from her nightstand, she slid her finger over the screen to answer when she saw who it was.

"Hey, Stacie," she said through another yawn.

"Hey, I didn't wake you did I? I assumed you'd be up by now."

"I'm still lying in bed but I woke up a few minutes ago, don't worry. What's going on?"

"Nothing much. Saturdays without you officially suck," Stacie huffed.

When they'd lived together, Saturday's had been their day together. Usually they spent it shopping at a local farmer's market or if they were feeling really motivated, they'd hit up the Navy Pier to have an early lunch and see a movie. "Then you just need to hop on a plane and get down here."

"Trust me, I'm working on it. I should have enough vacation time built up in two months to come stay for a week. That's not why I called though. You'll never guess who I saw last night."

"I haven't even had my coffee yet, I'm not guessing," she groaned.

Stacie sighed overdramatically. "Fine, you're no fun. After work last night I went out with some of the girls for happy hour and I saw none other than your ex, Dan, making out with someone who most definitely wasn't Amanda. When he saw me, he made a hasty exit. What an idiot. As if I'm going to tell your bitch ex-boss he's cheating on her too."

Carly couldn't help the small smile that spread across her face, even if it was a little mean. Karma could be a bitch sometimes. "I'm sure she'll see the light eventually." Or maybe not, Carly didn't really care.

"So how was your first week at work?"

"Ah…interesting."

"What's that tone?"

It was impossible to try hiding anything from her friend so Carly plunged ahead with the truth. "Well, there's no other way to say this except I slept with my boss last night."

"You didn't!"

"Oh, I *did*." And it had been amazing. She finger combed her tangled hair as she sat up. Oh yeah, she could practically feel Nick imprinted on her.

"This is the tall, hot, Greek guy right?"

"The one and only." Though that seemed like such a tame description of the man.

Stacie was silent for a moment then she snickered. "How was it?"

"Amazing. The best sex of my life actually."

"I can't believe it. This is so unlike you!"

"I know, right."

"Well, Miami certainly agrees with you… Crap, that's my other line. It's my sister so I've got to take it. I'll call you back this afternoon though. I want all the juicy details."

"Okay." Carly grinned as she hung up the phone. It was a week after Stacie's sister's due date and her family was just waiting for her to pop.

Easing off the bed, Carly stretched her legs as she stood. Her body was exquisitely sore thanks to Nick. He'd woken her twice during the night. Since he didn't have any more condoms, she thought they'd be through for the night, but he'd had no problem pleasuring her orally again and again. Hell, he'd been insistent. In her limited experience, that was a rare thing for a man. He almost seemed too good to be true.

A healthy dose of anxiety still played in the back of her head that things might get complicated since he was her boss, but it was easy to silence her worries with a man like Nick in her bed. Truthfully, it was easy to forget her own name with him around.

She glanced at the clock as she grabbed the silk robe she'd tossed over the chair sitting at her vanity. It was nine o'clock. After slipping on her robe, she descended the stairs in search of tall, dark and sexy. She didn't hear anything as she rounded the corner and walked toward the living room.

When she found the kitchen empty, her stomach dropped until she saw the spread of food on the round table. There was a box of fresh bagels and cream cheese from a nearby bakery, two bacon and cheese sandwiches, hot coffee—and a new box of condoms—but still no Nick. Laughing lightly, she picked up the box that proudly proclaimed it contained forty-eight lubricated, ribbed condoms. Well, they certainly wouldn't need the lubrication. The man got her wet just by looking at her.

"He must be feeling pretty sure of himself," she murmured to the empty room.

"I am." The enveloping deep timbre of Nick's voice caused her to drop the box. She swiveled to face him.

Pleasure speared through her when she realized he was completely naked. "Where'd you come from?" He'd come from the direction of the back door. Unless he'd been running around in her backyard naked, she couldn't imagine where he'd been.

As if he read her mind, he answered. "Your trash was full so I took it out."

"Naked?"

He shrugged as he walked toward her and ignored her question. "You hungry?"

"Wait, you went to the store this morning wearing clothing, right?" She tracked his long, muscular form as he headed for the bagels. She practically had to bite back a groan watching him move.

"Uh, yeah."

"So you took off your clothes once you got back and decided to go out in my grandmother's backyard, *naked*?"

Nick froze with his hand in the bagel box. "Shit. I didn't think about that."

Part of her thought it was a little odd that he didn't mind strolling around in the buff, but guys were so different. And if she had a body like that, she'd probably flaunt it too. "Thanks for picking up breakfast."

"I've got to keep you fed. Besides, you didn't have anything in your fridge. Want some coffee?"

When she nodded, he continued. "Take a seat. I'll fix it for you."

Carly did as he said, irrationally pleased he was getting her coffee. Watching him move around her kitchen while unabashedly naked was too surreal. She kept expecting to wake up and realize it was all a dream. That she'd just fantasized the whole interlude with Mr. Sexy.

The sound of her doorbell chime made them both pause.

Nick turned to face her, coffeepot in hand. "Expecting someone?"

"No." Shaking her head she stood and made sure the tie on her robe was secure before heading to the front door. After glancing through the peephole, she immediately tensed.

"Who is it?" Nick's voice was dangerously close to her ear.

Her heart jumped as she swiveled to face him. "How do you do that?" she whispered.

"What?"

"Sneak up on me...never mind. It's my grandmother so go hide," she whispered again.

He turned and disappeared down the hallway before she could tell him to go upstairs instead.

Her heart rate had kicked up, but she pasted a smile on her face and pulled the door open. After all, she was a grown woman. It didn't matter who she slept with. "Hey, Grandma."

Her grandmother smiled and kissed her on the cheek. "Hi, sweetie. I'm about to go meet some of the girls for breakfast but I wanted to let you know I saw a big dog running around the yard earlier so be careful. It looks dangerous."

"What kind of dog?"

"I don't know, but it was gray and white and almost looked like a wolf."

A shiver snaked down Carly's spine. "Thanks for letting me know."

"Are you still having dinner with me tonight?"

Crap. She'd completely forgotten. "Uh—"

"If you already have plans, don't worry. Mr. Lancaster asked me out to dinner but I told him I'd have to check with you first."

She placed a hand on her hip. "Who's Mr. Lancaster?"

Her grandmother mimicked her and lifted a haughty eyebrow. "Whose car is parked in the driveway?"

Carly's cheeks heated under her grandmother's knowing stare. "I'll come by later this afternoon, I promise," she mumbled.

"Don't bother, I'll probably be out. If you get a chance though, walk on over tomorrow for breakfast. Bring your friend if you want," she snickered before giving her another peck on the cheek.

Forget retirement, her grandmother had more of a social life than Carly did. After a quick glance around the yard, she shut and locked the front door.

When she returned to the kitchen she found Nick sitting at the kitchen table eating a bagel. She was disappointed to find him wearing boxers.

"Is everything okay?" he asked in between bites.

She took a seat and started smearing cream cheese on the blueberry bagel he'd laid out for her. "Yeah. My grandmother saw a big dog roaming around the yard earlier and wanted to let me know to be careful."

He shrugged. "I'm sure it's harmless."

She fought off a shudder. "I don't care. I hate dogs."

When Nick started choking on his food Carly popped up and rounded the table. She slapped him on the back a couple of times until he was breathing normally.

"Are you okay?" She stared down at him.

He cleared his throat and took a sip of coffee. "I'm fine. Guess it went down the wrong way. Uh, you hate dogs?"

"Hmm? Oh, well, I don't exactly *hate* them, but I don't go out of my way to befriend them." She picked up her bagel.

"Why?"

"When I was eight, a German shepherd attacked me." She stretched out her leg and twisted it so he could see the back of her calf. "You can't really see the scars anymore, but it was a horrible experience. I avoid dogs if I can."

"You don't like *any* dogs then, even puppies?" he asked incredulously.

She rolled her eyes. "Puppies are fine so don't start telling people I'm a puppy-hater. I just don't like the bigger breeds... Why, are you a dog person?"

He shrugged. "So, what are your plans for today?"

"I thought about going to the beach, but if you have something else in mind..." She crossed her legs, letting her robe fall open to expose most of her thighs.

Nick dropped the rest of his uneaten bagel onto his plate and his gaze darkened. "I was going to suggest we go to the Miami Seaquarium, but we can do that another day."

Carly tugged on the tie and let the silky material slide off her shoulders. "If you're sure."

CHAPTER EIGHT

Nick froze as Carly stripped down to nothing. She wasn't even wearing panties. His gaze narrowed in on the soft red strip of hair covering her mound and he could feel a growl begin deep in his throat.

The more he had her, the more he wanted her. He couldn't ever remember being so damn horny. It was as if someone else had taken over his body.

As he pushed up from his chair Carly uncrossed her legs, giving him a perfect view of her pussy. He grabbed her by the hands and hauled her up against him. She fit against his body as if they were two puzzle pieces, as if she'd been made just for him. The thought was ridiculous but he didn't care.

He crushed his mouth to hers while trailing his hands down her back to her perfect ass. He couldn't get enough of touching her. When he grabbed her cheeks and squeezed gently, she sighed into his mouth.

Last night had been torture not being able to fuck her again but now he was prepared. He tore his mouth away from hers and blindly reached for the condom box. After ripping the box open, he grabbed one of the packets and began to open it when she snatched it from his hands.

"My turn." Her smile was wicked as she peeled the packet open. When she fisted his pulsing cock in one of her slim hands, a shudder racked him.

Every time she touched him, he burned for her. It was as if she left a trail of fire in her wake. Instead of rolling the condom on him, however, she set it on the counter behind her and tugged his boxers down.

Before he realized what she planned, she'd kneeled in front of him and had taken the tip of his penis in her mouth. His hips jerked forward at the unexpected contact. When she ran her tongue along the underside of his shaft from the base back to the top, he threaded his fingers through her thick hair and groaned aloud. Ah, hell, it was exactly like his fantasy.

But she was better than any dream.

As she sucked and licked him, his knees started to buckle. God, her wicked mouth. Nick grasped the back of her head, forcing her to look up at him. "I want to be inside you." It was that primal thing driving him; that need to come inside her. It didn't matter that he'd be wearing a condom, he simply needed *in* her.

She moved to snag the condom, but he grabbed her by the hips, turned her around, and pushed her against the counter. It was the perfect height for what he had in mind. His inner wolf wanted to claim this female in the worst way possible.

"Stay still," he ordered, whispering against her ear.

Clutching the counter, she nodded as she looked at him over her shoulder. Then her smile turned pure wicked as she wiggled her ass at him.

It took all his control to get his damn condom on. He loved seeing her like this, bent over, spread open for him. But he needed her legs just a little wider. He spread them farther apart with his feet.

Her breathing became more erratic as he trailed a finger down her back and lower, lower, until he reached the crease of her cheeks. She tensed when he paused by her tight, rosy bud, but he kept going until he reached her slick folds.

With one finger, he probed inside her—and groaned. She was dripping wet and it was all for him. "This for me, baby?" He needed to hear her say it.

"Oh yeah." Her voice was a breathless whisper, the sexual energy rolling off her so damn strong it was like a physical blow.

Slowly, he pushed another finger in, savoring the feel of her clamping around him. A breathless groan escaped when he dragged his fingers against her inner walls. She was so tight.

"This isn't going to be gentle," he rasped out.

"I told you I won't break." She pushed back against him, the scent of her need wrapping around him and pushing him right to the edge of his control.

The lights in the kitchen were off, but there was enough natural light streaming in from the two windows that the room was incredibly bright.

Sunlight bathed Carly's body and reflected off the shiny hair tumbling down her back.

She was already wet enough and he simply didn't have the fortitude for any more foreplay. Last night he'd enjoyed tasting every inch of her but now he needed to feel her again. His entire body ached with the need.

Wordlessly he held onto her hips and plunged inside her.

She let out a yelp and arched her back at the sudden intrusion. He'd been worried about his size earlier, but she had no problem taking the full length of him.

For a moment he stayed where he was, buried balls-deep in Carly, letting her tight sheath squeeze around him.

He kept his hands on her hips and pressed his chest against the length of her back. "Touch yourself," he ordered. Just the thought or the sight of her teasing her clit or her breasts made his cock even harder.

As soon as the order was out of his mouth, she took both breasts in her hands and began palming them.

His cock pulsed with need as he watched her pinch and rub her nipples. From his position he didn't have a great view, but he knew she had the most perfect areolas. Pale pink that seemed even brighter against her ivory skin. And they got darker the more turned-on she was.

Though he was loath to pull out of her by even an inch, he finally began to move, to thrust harder and harder. With each stroke, she let out a purring sound, and it was all he could do not to come.

Each tortured moan she made pushed him closer to the edge. But he needed her to come first, was consumed with the hunger to feel her climax around his cock once again. Reaching around, he cupped her mound and flicked her clit with his thumb. She jerked at the small action, her breathing increasing.

As he slowly pushed in and out of her, he kept the pressure steady on her swollen bud. The harder she panted, the faster he moved his finger and his cock. When the walls of her pussy began locking around him, he clutched onto her hips and increased his pace.

For a moment he let his mental shield down and tapped into her mind. Pure pleasure hit him like a tidal wave. Her thoughts and feelings were too jumbled for him to make sense of anything, but she enjoyed what they were doing.

Her emotions were so strong they nearly knocked him over. He desperately wanted to link with her, to tell her what he was, but it was too soon.

He could bite her and she'd probably assume he was just a little kinky. But that would take away her choice about her future. He couldn't do that, no matter how much he ached to. And damn, he ached for a claiming. Only with Carly though.

Putting the shield back up, he pounded into her with a renewed frenzy. Her pussy fisted around his cock with startling intensity as she surged into orgasm. Her hands dropped from her breasts and clutched onto the edge of the counter. As she let out a low moan, he allowed himself to find his own release. His orgasm seemed to go on forever, her tight body wrenching every bit of pleasure from him.

Breathing hard, Carly leaned over the counter, barely moving. Sweat trickled down his face and back and after a few moments, he pulled out of her. His cock practically protested as he withdrew.

As he disposed of the condom, Carly picked up her silk robe and slid it on before collapsing on one of the chairs. He wished she'd just stay naked, but figured that wasn't going to happen. They'd never leave her place.

"Was I too rough?" He plucked his boxers from the floor.

Her pretty lips pulled up into a smile. "Stop worrying that I'm going to break."

Nick cupped her face in his hands and dropped a kiss on her forehead. "I can't help it. I take care of what's mine."

She might not realize it yet, but she was most definitely his.

* * *

"I've gotta say, you look pretty awesome on that bike." Carly snickered as Nick pulled to a stop next to her on the wide open sidewalk stretching down the oceanfront.

She'd convinced him to rent bikes and spend the day exploring the city. Not that it had taken much convincing. Spending Sunday with her like this was fucking heaven.

"I think that guy was lying about not having any other colors." They'd rented bikes at a local stand a few miles back and he'd ended up with a neon purple and blue one.

"It's still an awesome color. You make the purple more masculine."

Laughing, he swung his leg over and nodded at one of the food stands. The salty tinge of the nearby ocean teased the air, mixing with all the spicy aromas. "You hungry?"

"I could go for some ice cream." She got off her bike too and propped it next to his on a bench. "And I'm paying for it."

He ignored the last comment and slid an arm around her as they waited in line. There were only a couple people in front of them so they didn't have to wait long. Once they'd gotten their order they sat on the same bench they'd left their bikes.

"I'm having some dirty thoughts watching you lick that cone," he murmured, scooting closer to her.

"That's because you're a giant pervert." Smiling wickedly, she flicked her tongue over the top of it with slow deliberation.

Once again, he fought a groan. He couldn't walk around with a hard-on for her twenty-four-seven. Well he could, but he shouldn't. "Can't believe you got strawberry." With the ridiculous amount of selections, she'd surprised him with her choice.

"Strawberry is a classic. Plus, red hair? Come on."

A laugh rumbled from his chest as she grinned at him. Yep, he was falling so fast and so fucking hard for her he couldn't stop it if he wanted to. "Is that a rule that redheads like only strawberry?"

"No, but it's my excuse. You know you want some. I've seen you eyeing my ice cream."

"It's not the ice cream I'm watching."

She took another lick, this one slower, definitely more sensual. With her sunglasses on it was impossible to read her eyes, but her grin was all wicked.

"You'll pay for that later," he murmured.

"God, I hope so." She shifted against the bench seat, her navy blue shorts riding up just a bit, showing all that smooth skin he wanted to reach out and stroke. The scent of her desire was more than a little subtle.

He had to consciously ignore what it did to him, knowing she wanted him as much as he wanted her. His wolf clawed at him *again*, telling him to head back to her place so he could claim her. But he was enjoying this time with her.

"I was actually thinking of getting a bike," she continued. "It's too far to bike or walk to work, but it's so pretty where I live I figure I can find some nice places to ride."

"My cousin owns a sports shop not far from here. They've got a good selection of bikes. We can head there when we're done if you want." She would protest, but if she found something she liked, he'd get it for her.

"Let's do it. Would you mind terribly if we stopped by a craft store too? I checked my phone and there's one not too far from here."

If his brothers could see him, they'd laugh. He didn't care. "Sounds good to me. We have no solid plans today. Why'd you start knitting anyway?"

"Ah, well, it helped with everything after I lost my parents, gave me a creative outlet. At first anyway, now I really just enjoy it."

"Did you do the big throw in your living room?"

She nodded, taking another lick of her ice cream. Nick found himself jealous of an inanimate object.

"Yeah. Back in Chicago I was part of this group who made them for homeless shelters. We knitted tons of blankets and donated them. Eventually I started making baby clothes for a women's shelter near where I was living too. Once I get settled here I'm going to see if there are any knitting groups I can join... What? I know it's kind of a nerdy hobby."

He realized he was grinning when she trailed off and that she'd misunderstood his expression. "I just think it's adorable, that's all."

Her pretty mouth pulled into a frown. "Adorable? That's not what any woman wants to be called."

"Too bad, because you are—though you're still hot too." She was a combination of sweet and naughty. There was definitely something to be said for sweet women, something he should have realized years ago.

"Much better." She slid closer to him.

Without pause, he slung his arm around her shoulders and tossed his half-eaten cone into the nearby trashcan. Today was one of those perfect

Miami days. A few white clouds dotted the bright blue sky, and people biked, jogged, or walked their dogs as they passed by. He couldn't remember the last time he'd come down to the beach and enjoyed himself like this. Never with a woman. "Want to head down to the sand before we hit up the sport and craft stores?"

"You just want to see me in my bikini," she murmured, handing him her half-eaten cone as she laid her head on his shoulder. He tossed that one as well.

"You're not wrong."

She'd worn a tiny bikini under her shorts and tank top and yeah, he wanted to see her in it. Didn't matter that he'd seen her completely naked.

"I love how honest you are. And it doesn't matter to me. I'm enjoying sitting right here with you."

"Me too... My ancestors are originally from Leontio," he said, abruptly changing the subject. He'd actually been born there but he couldn't tell her that.

"That's in Greece I'm assuming?"

"Yep."

"Have you been there?"

"Oh yeah. Leontio's a little mountain village. I've been thinking about heading back for a vacation later this year." And he wanted to bring her with him. He wasn't sure why it was so important, but his inner wolf wanted it as well. By then he hoped to have told her exactly what he was.

"That'll be fun." Her voice was slightly drowsy and though he couldn't see, he guessed her eyes were closed as she leaned against him.

"You should come with me." The words were out before he could think about censoring himself.

She lifted her head. "Are you serious?"

He shrugged. It was too soon to be talking about anything like that, but... "Yeah."

She watched him for a long moment and he wished he could see her eyes. "If anyone else said that, I'd think it was a line."

"I don't need any more lines to get in your pants."

Laughing, she pinched his side and stood. "You're right about that. Come on, let's get out of here before I fall asleep on your shoulder."

He followed suit, getting on his bike when she got on hers. She'd never answered his question. Well, he hadn't actually asked, he'd just said she should go with him. It was too soon for her, especially since she was a human. Not for him though; his wolf and human side were in complete agreement about sexy Carly Kendall. She belonged with him.

CHAPTER NINE

Carly glanced away from the computer screen and shook her head. It was almost noon and she hadn't completed even half of what needed to be done today. All she could focus on was the past weekend with Nick. The sex had been amazing, but she'd also had a lot of fun with him. He was so relaxing to be around—and so incredibly sweet. He'd even bought her a new bike. She hadn't wanted to let him, but he'd been insistent and his cousin had refused to let her pay anyway. It was weirdly awesome to have a guy want to take care of her and be so attentive.

Now she couldn't concentrate on anything. Couldn't keep her mind off the toe- curling sex she'd been having and the wonderfulness of Nick. It almost felt as if she were living someone else's life. A sexy man built like a god who liked giving oral sex more than he liked receiving it did not just fall into her lap.

"Hey, looks like someone's back in the dating game." Alex's voice from the open doorway caused her to glance up.

Carly frowned at the vase of blood-red roses in Alex's hands. There were at least two dozen in the bouquet. "What's that?"

The other woman shrugged as she placed them on the desk. "Someone just delivered them. No note, just your name on a white card."

Carly bit her bottom lip. She and Nick had discussed keeping their relationship private, at least until they figured out where things were going. In reality, she was the one who'd insisted. He didn't seem to care who knew about them but she'd just started working here and didn't want everyone talking about her. She couldn't believe he'd sent her flowers—and freaking roses at that—after the talk they'd had. Even if it was sweet.

Before she could respond, Nick strolled in. A frown marred his face the second he spotted the bouquet. "What's that?"

Alex looked back and forth between Nick and Carly, grinning. "Someone sent Carly flowers. Wonder who it could be," she sang as she walked out.

"Did you tell her about us?" Carly whispered once Alex was gone and out of earshot.

"No. Who are those from?" he growled.

She blinked. "They're not from you?"

His pale gaze darkened as he stared at the bouquet. "No."

"Oh." She plucked the simple white card from the holder and turned it over. Alex was right, it was blank except for her name. "That's weird." Shrugging, she met Nick's gaze. "I don't really like roses, but they're really pretty anyway."

Instead of responding, he stared at the flowers with a heated gaze, as if he thought he could destroy them with lightning bolts from his eyes.

"Uh, you okay?" she asked.

"Fine. Do you want to take lunch with me today?"

"Do you think it's such a good idea?"

"I told you, Carly. I don't care if—"

"Hey, big brother!" The man Carly had seen at Friday's party, the one who looked similar to Nick, strolled into the office and slapped Nick on the back.

"Hey, what are you doing here?" Nick's entire body was tense, but his expression softened for his brother.

"I stopped by to..." Carly watched in fascination as Nick's brother stopped and sniffed the air. Kind of like a dog would. Then he slapped his brother on the back again. He glanced back and forth between Nick and Carly with a big grin on his face, as if expecting them to say something.

She raised her eyebrows at Stephan, but tried not to stare too hard. Nick's brother might be acting a little strange, but she didn't want to insult Nick.

"Meet me in the garage." Nick's words came out as a tight order.

Chuckling, his brother left the small office.

"What was that about?" she whispered.

Nick shook his head. "Don't worry about it. My brother works odd hours and sometimes doesn't get any sleep for days. He's just tired. About lunch—"

"I don't think it's a good idea, Nick." At his frown she continued. "Not yet anyway. I want to see where this thing goes. I just started working here and people will talk if we start spending lunches together."

"What about tonight?"

"What about it?"

"Do you have plans?"

"No."

"You do now. We can go out or I'll cook for you."

She bit back a grin. "That sounds suspiciously like an order."

He cleared his throat and spoke in much softer tones. "Ah, would you like to have dinner with me tonight?"

"Yes. You can pick me up at seven. And I don't care if we go out or not." That would give her enough time to get home, freshen up and clear her brain. She'd lived and breathed Nick the past couple days and her mind and body needed to decompress. She was falling for him so fast and it was a little terrifying. She could see a real future with the sexy man. When she'd moved here she hadn't even been thinking of dating or men and now she had a perfect one. That just didn't happen.

Nick nodded and left. As she turned her attention back to the computer screen, her cell phone rang. She hadn't given her new number out to many people so she couldn't imagine who was calling.

Even though she didn't recognize the number, it was a Miami area code so Carly answered in case it was her grandmother calling from a different phone. "Hello?"

"Hi, is this Carly?"

The voice sounded vaguely familiar. "Yes, who is this?"

"It's Dennis."

"Who?"

"Dennis Chontos, from Friday's party." His voice held a trace of barely concealed annoyance.

Who? "Oh, right. How are you?" She'd forgotten about him. They'd talked maybe a total of five minutes before Nick had dragged her away. Not that she was complaining.

"I'm great. You left before I got a chance to get your number—"

"Yeah, exactly how did you get my number?"

"From Alex."

"Oh." Annoyance flickered through her. That didn't sound like Alex, but Carly supposed she didn't really know her well enough to make that call.

"Anyway, I wanted to take you out sometime. Are you free this weekend?"

She glanced toward the open doorway, suddenly feeling guilty, even though she'd done nothing wrong. "No, I'm actually seeing someone."

"Alex said you were single." His abrupt, almost rude statement sent a chill down her spine. It wasn't his words so much as his domineering tone.

"We just started seeing each other."

He completely ignored her statement. "Did you get the flowers I sent you?"

"Oh, I didn't realize who they were from. Listen, thank you for the flowers but I'm at work so I have to go." She disconnected before he could respond.

She was probably being paranoid, but she didn't like the fact that someone she didn't know had sent flowers to her place of employment and gotten her phone number without asking her for it first. It was just plain weird. Since she'd practically hung up on him, he'd no doubt gotten the hint.

* * *

Asha clenched his cell phone tightly in his hand. He resisted the urge to slam it against the kitchen counter. The stupid bitch was lying to him. She wasn't seeing anyone. Even if she was fucking that lycan from the party, he hadn't marked her, which meant she was fair game.

His skin practically itched at the woman's rejection. Women never said no to him. She was the perfect blend of innocence and sexuality. As long as he had steady sex, he could keep his power up so it wasn't even that he needed her. No, he wanted this one.

After pouring himself a healthy glass of scotch, he stalked up the stairs. His slave had been unusually quiet all morning. He allowed her to watch television and work out, but in the last hour he hadn't heard any movement. He'd been a little rough with her last night so maybe she'd fallen asleep.

Glancing around his dark room, he frowned to discover it empty.

"Slave, come here!"

When she didn't respond, he headed for the small workout room at the end of the hallway. It was empty.

She couldn't have escaped. Of that, he was sure. With bulletproof, reinforced windows and biometric scanners on all the exits, it was next to impossible for anyone to enter or leave without his knowledge. And none of the motion sensors outside had been triggered.

He walked back to his massive room and opened the bathroom door. His lips curled up in disgust. The woman's head fell to the side unnaturally and her silky blonde hair fell over the side of the clawfoot tub. Splatters of crimson covered the tile floor and white walls.

He cursed when he saw the broken mirror.

Careful to step around the shards of glass, he strode across the room. Though he hated to get his hands dirty, he reached into the brackish water and pulled the plug. As the water decreased, he could see the jagged wounds slicing across her wrists.

"Stupid bitch," he muttered. Now he'd have to clean up the mess and dispose of her body.

Not to mention he'd be without sex for a few days. If he got desperate, he could find a prostitute, but he preferred his women to look clean and innocent.

Now he knew it was fate that the redhead had fallen into his path. One way or another, the woman would be his.

* * *

Nick scowled at Stephan as he stalked across the garage toward him. "What the hell was that? You were sniffing Carly's office like a mangy dog."

His brother simply grinned and leaned against the Mercedes Nick had been working on all morning. "Whatever, I didn't expect to walk in and smell your fucking scent everywhere. Good God man, did you fuck all weekend?"

Nick took a steadying breath. He knew his brother wasn't trying to get under his skin. "It's more than that."

Stephan snorted. "I kind of guessed. Does she know... about the family?"

"No, and I plan to keep it that way for a while."

Stephan nodded. "I understand."

He sighed and scrubbed a hand over his face. "There's more to it than the whole shifter thing. She hates dogs, man."

His brother let out a loud bark of laughter, which just annoyed Nick. "Are you serious?"

"Yep. She was attacked when she was a kid. She's afraid of them."

"Damn."

"I know. It's not that big of a deal but it's going to be hard enough telling her without this added." The world was full of shifters, fairies, Immortals, and even a few vampires were still around, but most humans weren't aware of their existence.

"You going to tell her before you bond with her?"

"Yes." Not only did he have to tell her he was a werewolf, but he also had to tell her that she was his mate. And that would just bring up a dozen other issues they had to deal with. If she didn't run screaming when he admitted what he was, of course. Over the weekend he'd almost bonded with her a couple times, but he'd managed to control his inner wolf. Barely. His freaking wolf was getting cranky and possessive.

"What's the sex like? I've heard that when it's your mate, it's—"

"What's up with all the questions?" he snapped.

His brother shoved his hands in his pockets. "I've been waiting as long as you have, man. I just wanted to know if it's like all the stories we heard growing up."

Guilt swept through Nick. A lot of werewolves found their mates, but many never did. Their parents had been lucky and it was something Nick had wished to experience for longer than he cared to admit. Neither of his brothers had said anything but he knew they felt the same way. They were extraordinarily lucky because they had their family to depend on. Sure they moved every couple of decades to a new city to hide their slower aging, but their pack was large and supportive. Not all shifters had that.

"I'm sorry, my head's all messed up."

Stephan shrugged and pushed up from the car. "I've got to go anyway. Just a heads-up, Mom and Dad will be back tomorrow."

"Thanks," he said as his brother left. That was just one more thing he didn't want to worry about. He and his brothers were born alphas, but as things stood, his father was the current Alpha of their pack so he'd have to introduce Carly. It wasn't a question of not wanting to—or having a choice really—but he knew how pushy his family was and he didn't want them forcing anything on her until she was ready.

* * *

Carly waited for the hum of her computer to stop before she pushed her chair back and stood up. She glanced at her flowers as she arranged her desk. Nick had been coming in all day and staring at the stupid arrangement with barely concealed disgust.

Even though they were pretty, she plucked them out of the vase and walked out of her office toward the lobby. She didn't see anyone in the garage so she headed out the front door and rounded the building until she found the Dumpster. Sighing at the waste, she tossed them into the garbage and went back to her office.

The small room had a long way to go before she'd be satisfied with the way it looked, but for now she could at least straighten things.

As she bent over the desk, two hands slid around her waist. For a split second she tensed until Nick's familiar scent tangled around her. She leaned back into his chest, trying to control her erratic breathing while she savored his earthy, spicy, smell. "What are you doing?"

He feathered her neck with kisses before turning her around to face him. "You ready to get out of here?"

"I thought you were picking me up at seven." She tried to take a step back but the desk stopped her.

"I could or we could start right here," he murmured before nipping her bottom lip between his teeth.

As always around him, heat pooled between her legs at his near proximity. "We can't do anything at work. Anyone could walk in—"

"Everyone's gone home and I've already locked up."

Well wasn't he just prepared? She tried to think of another argument, but came up short. It wasn't that she didn't enjoy being around him, because she did—probably too much—but everything was happening so fast. Maybe too fast. It was hard to get a handle on the sudden onslaught of emotions she'd undergone since meeting him. She'd dated her ex for almost a year and hadn't felt one iota of the attraction she had for Nick. It wasn't even in the same stratosphere.

And that scared the holy hell out of her. Even as regret pulsed through her, she lightly pushed on his chest. "Let's do this another time."

"You don't want me to come over tonight?" Though his expression was neutral, there was an undercurrent of hurt rolling off him.

"What... no, I still want you to. I just don't want to do...anything *here*." Okay, she kind of did, but just not today.

The tightness in his shoulders loosened. Nick dropped a chaste kiss on her forehead and took a step back, giving her the space she'd said she wanted. "I'll see you in a couple hours then."

She nodded as she hooked her purse over her shoulder and made her way to the front door. Carly could feel his gaze penetrating her back as she walked, but she refused to turn around. Once she slid into the front seat of her car, she saw him watching her through the lobby window. Thankfully her car started right away. Whatever he'd done to it last week, it now ran better than ever.

She half waved as she pulled out of the parking lot. Once she was on the road, she felt more in control of herself. If she didn't get a couple of hours of time to herself she was afraid she'd fall completely for Nick. And something told her he wasn't the kind of man to be tied down permanently. Sure, he'd made that comment about her going with him to Greece, but it was hard to believe he'd been serious. She needed to gain back some control before she did something really stupid. Like lose her heart.

CHAPTER TEN

Nick put his car in park but didn't get out immediately. He stared at Carly's little one-bedroom apartment and tried to get himself together. He couldn't figure out what had changed between them but it was obvious something had. She'd practically shoved him off her at the office. Okay, maybe it hadn't been that extreme, but human females were a lot more complex than shifter females. He'd scented Carly's desire. Still, she'd pushed him away and he didn't understand why.

More than anything he wanted to get into her head but he couldn't invade her privacy like that. Not if they stood a chance to build a future. He might be relationship challenged, but even he knew that much about women. If he broke her trust now, he'd be screwed for years to come.

Sighing to himself, he grabbed the two overflowing grocery bags and walked toward the front door. It swung open before he'd knocked.

"I saw you drive up. What's all this?" Carly tried to take one of the bags from him, but he held it firm.

"I'm cooking for you." Without staring too hard, he drank in her appearance and tried to tamp down his desire. She'd changed into skimpy pink beach shorts and a white tank top and looked good enough to eat. All that skin on display just for him. His inner wolf flared to the surface, clawing and demanding he claim this female right now.

Her eyes brightened as she peered inside the bag closest to her. "What are you making?"

"Moussaka." It was his mother's recipe and it dated back many years. He'd never cooked it for another woman before. Had never wanted to until Carly.

She grinned as she shut the front door. "I love moussaka. There was a Greek restaurant on the same block where I worked in Chicago. I used to eat there a couple times a week."

That was one thing in his favor. She might hate dogs but at least she liked Greek food. "Have you ever made it before?" he asked.

She snorted as they entered the kitchen. "There's something you should know about me right now. I don't cook. If it wasn't for my grandmother, I'd probably starve."

"I'll just have to teach you then," he said as he set the bags onto the counter.

She shook her head. "It won't help, trust me. My grandmother has tried to teach me. I don't think I have a knack for it."

"We'll see." He pulled out a clear plastic bag full of eggplants and glanced around the kitchen. There wasn't a knife block anywhere. "Uh, knives?"

Carly pulled open the drawer closest to the sink and pointed inside. He frowned at the blunt knives. For now he could use them, but he was getting her some new utensils in the near future. How did someone not have a knife block?

"Is that what you need?"

"This'll work." He pulled out one of the knives and grabbed the cutting board he'd seen hidden behind her bread box.

"So what are you doing exactly?" She peered over his shoulder as he started slicing the eggplants.

"Cutting these into thin enough slices. Then I'll salt them and we'll wait until the salt pulls the moisture out."

Her brows furrowed as she looked at the vegetables. "Do you want something to drink? I've got beer."

"Actually I brought some wine if you don't mind grabbing it from the other bag. It's chilled but it'll need to go in the refrigerator."

She pulled the bottle from the bag and read the label. "Malamatina Retsina."

"It's light. I think you'll like it."

Carly might not use her kitchen for cooking, but she'd still decorated the room. It was set up in a retro style with no overhead cabinets. Instead, shelves displayed bowls, wineglasses and other stemware. She pulled two delicate-looking glasses from the shelf nearest the sink and poured drinks for them.

She set his glass next to him and took a sip from her own as she leaned against the counter mere inches away. His wolf clawed again, wanting a taste of her.

"Was everything okay with your brother? You seemed stressed after he left today."

"Yeah, just family stuff." Talking about his family wasn't something he ever did. The Lazos pack had integrated well into every city they moved to but there was always a certain amount of distance they kept from people. Hell, he hadn't even been able to tell Carly he'd been born in Greece. Instead he'd had to tell her he'd grown up in Miami.

Lying to his intended mate left a foreign feeling of sickness inside him. Of course, he had more important things to worry about. Like figuring out how to tell her he was a shifter. If he moved too soon, he'd scare her away. "Listen, I was wondering if you wanted to have dinner with my family tomorrow night. It'll be like the party on Friday. Lots of food and people."

"Sure." Smiling, she took another sip.

Obviously she didn't understand he meant his parents would be there and he chose not to elaborate. Yeah, it was a total chickenshit thing to do but until he could figure out what had caused her to suddenly pull away from him, he wasn't giving her more ammunition to run. After the weekend they'd had, he hadn't thought she'd have a reason to, but something was off. He wished he could put his finger on what it was.

Slicing the eggplant was the easiest part of the meal. A few moments later, he laid out the pieces onto paper towels and salted them.

"Do you need help with anything?" Carly still hadn't moved from her spot as she watched him.

"Nope. Now we wait."

"Wait?"

"Mmm hmm. For about half an hour. What can we do for thirty minutes to pass the time?" He dried his hands off on one of the dishrags and plucked the wineglass from her hand.

Her cheeks had turned that adorable shade of pink and even though he sensed she was uneasy, desire rolled off her in potent waves. Nick placed both hands on the counter next to her, effectively caging her in. He leaned down until he was a few inches from her face. The sweet smell of wine tickled his nose, but nothing was sweeter than her natural scent. "What's going on in that pretty head of yours, Carly?"

"What do you mean?" she rasped out, her fingers skating over his chest.

His cock jumped when she moistened her lips. "What's changed between us since this weekend?"

"Everything's happening so fast."

"Yeah." *So what?* Everything he knew about her, he liked. Maybe more than just liked. Which sounded stupid in his head, but he didn't care.

"Well, maybe we jumped into this without thinking." There was a note of unease in her voice that sliced at him.

"I don't regret anything."

"Neither do I."

"Then what's the problem?"

She shrugged, but when she nervously tucked a strand of hair behind her ear, he understood what was going on. "I'm not looking for a fling, Carly. Are you?"

"No," she answered quickly, smoothing out some of his raw edges.

Nick leaned a little closer. "Then what else is wrong?"

"Like I said, everything is happening so fast. I don't..."

"You don't what?"

"We haven't known each other that long, but every time you touch me, it's like my body heats up about a hundred degrees and I just can't think straight. You seem almost too perfect."

That was exactly how he felt about her. "And that's a bad thing?"

"No. Definitely not. I've just never had such a physical response to anyone."

"Does it scare you?"

She bit her bottom lip. "A little."

Nick wasn't sure how to respond. Their chemistry was off the charts so he wasn't sure what the problem was. When her bright gaze focused on his mouth, her lips parted slightly. He wasn't sure if she was going to say anything, but he took away anything she might have been contemplating. Hell, she was lucky he'd held off touching her this long.

The need to be touching her, inside her, was all consuming.

Soft lips met his with heated intensity. Whatever her insecurities, they didn't extend to the physical aspect of their relationship. Her heart slammed against her ribs like a jackhammer and he could feel it as clearly as if it was his own pounding heart.

He slid his hands up under the bottom of her shirt so he could feel her bare skin. Skin to skin touching was important to shifters. He shuddered as he wrapped his hands around her ribs. She was slim, but not emaciated like so many of the women that frequented his brother's club. Just enough curves and she fit perfectly against him.

Carly apparently forgot whatever had been bothering her as she hurriedly tugged at the bottom of his shirt. As long as they were touching and she wasn't overthinking, they seemed to be in sync. He stepped back and yanked it off before quickly seeking out her mouth again. If it was up to him, they'd both just go naked whenever they were at her place or his. Not that he'd taken her there yet, but soon.

Her lips were soft and pliant underneath his demanding kisses. His cock pressed painfully against his jeans when she slid her hands up his chest and dug her nails into his shoulders. He'd been thinking about this all day; had been unable to stop himself from dropping into her office just to say hi.

As she moaned against his mouth, her entire body lined up flush against his. That sweet raspberry scent enveloped him to the point he wanted to scrape his teeth across Carly's neck and leave his mark. But he didn't. He couldn't. Not if he wanted to live with himself. She deserved better than that.

Somehow he tore his hands away from her soft skin and tangled with the button on her shorts. As he unzipped them, they slid down her long legs and pooled at her feet. Seconds later, her bright yellow thong followed, revealing the small tuft of red hair covering her mound. He couldn't wait to bury his face between her legs.

Clutching her hips, he lifted her up onto the edge of the counter before using his hands to open her legs further.

"What are you doing?" she whispered.

"What do you think, sweetheart?" Without pause, he knelt in front of her and kissed the inside of her leg right by her knee. He was tall enough that he was at the perfect position to pleasure her this way.

Her legs started to close on his head so he placed a firm hand on one of her thighs. "Relax," he murmured. When he met her gaze, desire burned bright in her blue eyes. Satisfied with her response, he kissed her again, this time higher.

Trailing kisses up her leg, he took his time as he created a path toward her pussy. The folds of her lips were swollen and her pink clit peeked out, begging him to lick her everywhere. After this past weekend, he knew exactly how much pressure to use, how to make her come against his mouth.

The anticipation was almost too much.

Inhaling her sweet scent, he teased her lips, tracing his tongue up the outermost part of her folds. Her breathing hitched as he reached her clit, but he barely flicked his tongue over it. He didn't want to focus all his energy there. Not yet. Not when he knew it would drive her crazy if he prolonged this.

For a moment, he pulled back and simply stared at her. Her pink folds were so fucking perfect it almost pained him to look away. Hell, everything about her was perfect.

Sighing, he leaned forward and delved as deeply as he could with his tongue. Her sweet slickness coated him and it took all his control not to strip off his pants and slide his cock into her. When she moaned and threaded her fingers through his hair his balls pulled up even tighter.

"More." The word was barely above a whisper, but he heard it as clearly as if she'd spoken directly into his ear. That was another sign he knew she was his mate. No matter what he could hear and feel everything she was.

Driving his tongue deeper, he shuddered when he could actually feel her inner walls tremble and contract around him.

By her uneven breathing and the loud thump of her heartbeat, he knew she wanted more from him. All shifters had extrasensory abilities, but as a werewolf, his hearing was even more acute. Her heart sounded as if it would jump out of her chest.

And he knew exactly how to bring her to a quick climax. He'd planned to drag this out longer, but he shifted slightly and inserted two fingers into her tight sheath. He didn't stop kissing her though. As he ran his tongue around her clit, her inner walls convulsed rapidly.

"Right there," she murmured as her hands moved to his shoulders.

He dragged his fingers against her inner walls, earning a shudder from her. She was dripping wet and tight as hell. When she tried to move her hips against his hand, he pushed back into her then pulled out again, increasing his momentum with each stroke.

As he continued thrusting into her wet sheath, he barely grazed her aroused bud with his tongue. Everywhere he licked tasted sweet. The faster he moved, the quicker she contracted around his fingers.

The scent of her arousal and impending release hit him with a startling force. Instead of teasing her, he sucked her clit into his mouth. Her entire body jolted at the tug. When she surged into climax he could actually feel her pleasure shooting through to all his nerve endings. That was how connected they were.

Carly's stomach muscles bunched as an orgasm rocked through her. Somehow, Nick knew every nuance of her body. Knew exactly where to touch and kiss her, guaranteeing she found release every time.

Which only served to confuse her more. He was so intent on pleasuring her all the time, but she was afraid he might be too good to be true. A man who cooked and knew how to bring her to climax with a few strokes was a fantasy. Not to mention she felt this strange connection to him that she couldn't explain, even to herself. It was as if she'd known him forever, and not just a week.

As she came down from her high, he stood and pulled her close to him in a comforting embrace. He was silent as his strong arms enveloped her. She wrapped her legs around his waist and laid her head against his chest. His heart thundered, but he made no move to indicate that he wanted any more from her.

Well, she definitely wanted more. Wordlessly she leaned back and tugged at his belt, but almost instantly he placed his hands over hers, stilling them.

"This was about you, Carly, not me." His deep voice had the oddest soothing effect on her nerves.

Even so, she batted his hands away and finished unfastening his belt. This relationship wasn't one-sided. "The hell it is. Do you have any condoms on you?"

He paused, as if he might argue, but instead he grabbed one from his pocket then let his pants fall around his ankles. As he ripped open the packet, she pulled her tank top over her head. He'd been in such a frenzy earlier he hadn't bothered with her shirt, but right now she wanted to feel his chest against hers. The skin to skin contact with him made her crazy.

With his hand firmly at the base of his cock, he stopped after he'd rolled the condom on and stared at her. The way he seemed to drink her in with his eyes was an aphrodisiac by itself. No man had ever looked at her like that.

Like she was truly special. Beautiful even. He really seemed to care too, wanting to know everything about her.

She scooted closer to the edge of the counter and wrapped her arms around his back. Her hands had a mind of their own as they searched out his firm ass and squeezed. The man had a body so fine-tuned he would put Greek gods to shame.

He didn't need more of an invitation than that. Nick drove into her and at the same time, crushed his mouth over hers in that frantic, now-familiar way of his. Even though she was already slick, an involuntary gasp escaped as he buried his cock in her.

She loved the way he stretched and filled her. She barely had enough time to catch her breath as he pulled out and slammed into her again. His arm and neck muscles corded so tightly she could see the tendons stretch and pulse as he moved. This time there was nothing gentle about their coupling. He grabbed her hips and pistoned into her again and again.

His grip on her was sure to leave bruises, but she didn't care. Carly tightened her legs around him as he moved, meeting him stroke for stroke. Every time he slammed into her, her breasts brushed against his chest. The coarse hair sprinkled across his chest rubbed her nipples, teasing the already sensitized buds.

She could barely breathe as he ate at her mouth, devouring her with kisses. As he tugged on her bottom lip with his teeth she nearly came undone. Her body was undergoing too many sensations at once. All because of sweet, delicious Nick.

When he moved his mouth to her jaw and neck those feelings intensified even more. He scraped his teeth across her neck, the roughness of it pushing her over the edge.

Finally she let go of the small modicum of control she'd been trying to hold onto. A tiny orgasm rippled through her. It was nothing compared to the one earlier, but the pleasant surprise had her clutching onto Nick's shoulders as her pussy clamped around his cock.

Nick let out a loud groan as he buried himself inside her one last time. His groan almost sounded like a roar it was so intense. She wasn't sure how long they held each other afterward, but she didn't mind his solid embrace.

Carly was too tired to move. Hell, too tired to think, really. Two orgasms back-to-back were a bit much. Her toes were numb and her skin was super-sensitized.

Nick eventually loosened his viselike grip on her hips and immediately she missed the connection.

"Birth control." His face was nuzzled against her neck, muffling his words, but she thought she'd understood what he'd said.

"Hmm?"

Still breathing hard, Nick lifted his head and pressed his forehead against hers. "Have you ever been on the Pill?"

She nodded. It had been a while since she'd needed to be so she'd simply stopped taking her pills.

"Will you go on it again? I'll pay for everything."

"Yes, but you don't have to do that." Her words came out as a breathy whisper. How he could talk, much less think was beyond her. She unlocked her legs from behind his waist and stretched them out. She tried wiggling her toes to get some feeling back in them.

"Of course I do," he rumbled.

What? Oh right, birth control. Well, she wasn't going to argue with him. "I'll set up an appointment next week."

He nipped her bottom lip in response.

As her breathing subsided she realized the picture they must paint and a giggle escaped.

"You're laughing while I'm still inside you?" His lips twitched slightly as he watched her.

To her horror, another laugh escaped. "I'm sorry. It's just that I'm naked, your pants are around your ankles and your boots are still on."

An unexpected grin broke across his face, stealing all her breath. God, if he smiled more often, he'd be absolutely irresistible to women everywhere. The smile completely transformed his face. His mouth turned up, revealing an almost perfect row of white teeth and he had a tiny dimple on his left cheek she'd never noticed before.

No longer was he formidable and intimidating. Sure, he still had that authoritative presence, but his relaxed features gave him an almost boyish, charming quality. In reality, there was nothing remotely boyish about Nick. No, he was all man. Every toned, muscled inch of him. Still, that smile...all he'd have to do was turn on the charm and she'd do anything he wanted. A shiver of desire slid up her spine and her nipples beaded even more. Heck, she'd do pretty much anything he wanted right now.

"You should definitely smile more often," she said.

"I smile." The words were almost defensive.

"Hmm. Says you." She poked her forefinger against his chest, forcing him to take a step back so she could hop off the counter. "I need to put some clothes on and you promised to feed me."

A small grin played at the corners of his mouth as he discarded the condom and pulled his jeans back up. "After dinner I hope you're ready for more dessert."

"More?" Her belly clenched as she slid her shorts on.

"You better believe it."

Her legs were weak and tingly but she could handle another round soon enough. Still, they needed to talk about something besides sex or they'd never make it to dinner before she jumped him again. "So, how long have you been working on cars?"

"Since I got my '68 Dodge Charger." His words were laced with undeniable pride.

"Well, that doesn't tell me much because I seriously doubt you got it new off the assembly line."

He glanced at her and for a second he looked confused. The expression disappeared almost immediately. "Ah, since I was a teenager. I'd had it about a year when it started giving me engine trouble. It took a little while to figure things out, but ever since then, I've been a car man."

"It's definitely a hot car. I bet it gave you a leg up with the ladies in school." Not that he would need it.

He just shot her a quick, wicked grin as he started emptying one of the paper bags.

She picked up her glass of wine and took a few sips. She'd never thought watching a man cook would be sexy. Especially not a man like Nick. Everything about him was big and, well, masculine. He should look out of place in her small kitchen, but he moved around as if he'd always been there.

"What about you? You never told me why you moved to Miami other than for your grandmother.

I got the feeling there might be more to it." Nick's voice cut through her thoughts.

"Well…" For a second she thought about lying, but then decided against it. There was no reason she couldn't be honest about her ex-boyfriend. It still got under her skin that he'd cheated on her but that was his problem, not hers. "There wasn't one reason in particular. I found out my ex-boyfriend was cheating on me…" She cleared her throat, trying to decide if this fell in the too-much-information-at-once department, but plunged ahead. "With my old boss. Since my grandmother lives here, I figured why not? I needed a change and I had a place to stay. And so far, Miami is kicking Chicago's ass."

His mouth tugged up at the corners at her last statement, but he shook his head as he pulled an onion out of one of the paper bags. "I can't imagine any man cheating on you."

The sincerity of his words touched her in a way she hadn't realized she'd needed to hear. It wasn't a line and he obviously wasn't trying to get anything out of her. He didn't *need* lines to get her into bed. He was just stating a simple fact.

She set her wineglass down and nudged him with her hip. "I'll chop these and you do whatever it is you need to do."

He handed her the knife and glanced around the kitchen. "You have a frying pan right?"

She bit her bottom lip. "I think so."

He groaned as he bent down to pull open the drawer underneath the stove. She cringed when he pulled out an old skillet that she knew wasn't hers. It wasn't dirty, but the plastic on the handle was chipping and it looked like it was about twenty years old. Must have belonged to her grandmother's last tenant.

"Will that work?" She nodded at the pan.

He nodded and chuckled. "It'll work for now, but I'm buying you a new set of pots and pans."

"You can't keep buying me stuff." She'd never been with a man so insistent on taking care of her. When he said he'd buy her pans, she knew it wasn't an empty promise, especially after the four hundred dollar bike. The thought of him spending that kind of money made her cringe a little. Her ex had occasionally paid for her when they went out to eat but he'd been all about splitting things fifty-fifty. It had always bugged her that he'd never taken the time to wine and dine her or even try to impress her really.

He didn't bother turning around from the counter. "We'll just see about that."

Dating a man like Nick Lazos could turn out to be very addictive. She still hadn't decided if that was a good or bad thing.

CHAPTER ELEVEN

Carly sighed as Nick massaged her shoulders and the powerful shower jets pummeled the front of her body. "We're going to be late to work."

"Considering I'm the boss, it doesn't matter." Nick's hands left her shoulders and strayed to her waist. One hand slid around her middle as he pulled her back against his chest. She could feel his heart beating triple time.

Even though they'd already made love once, he was still rock hard, something she should be used to by now. His hips shifted and his cock rubbed against her backside. "You can just forget it," she said without turning around.

"Forget what?" he murmured close to her ear, his voice low and intoxicating.

It was *almost* enough to weaken her resolve but she took a step forward, twisted the shower knob to off and turned to face him. She looked at his cock, then moved back up to his face. "You know exactly what I'm talking about."

He almost looked like a frustrated child as he grabbed her hips. "Who cares if we're late?"

She'd never had sex this amazing and the thought of another bout of lovemaking was more than tempting, but she forced herself to stand her ground. "*I care.* I don't want anyone knowing about us yet. I swear Alex knows anyway and if we both show up late, it'll look strange. Besides, I don't want any preferential treatment."

His lips pulled into a thin line as he dragged the black, white and pink damask shower curtain back. The hooks jangled loudly against the rod, a mirror of his annoyance. Instead of responding, he handed her a towel before grabbing one and wrapping it around his waist.

They hadn't even been seeing each other a week so she couldn't understand why he was upset. Yeah, she liked him a lot, and yes, she could really see this thing going somewhere, but she didn't want to jinx it. She might have had a few twinges of doubt about his intentions but after last night it was obvious he wasn't looking for a fling. Still, that didn't mean she wanted to shout from the rooftops that she was sleeping with her *boss*. Because if things went south it would be beyond embarrassing if everyone at work knew about it.

When he looked at her, his jaw clenched in annoyance before he disappeared into the bedroom. Sighing, she wrapped her towel around her and picked up her comb. As soon as she'd finished brushing the tangles from her hair, he stepped back into the bathroom already fully dressed.

"I'm going to head in now." He had that annoyingly neutral expression in place.

"You don't want to have breakfast together?" It was stupid to feel hurt, but she couldn't help the disappointment in her voice.

"Don't want to be late." She didn't miss the subtle trace of sarcasm in his voice.

"Fine." She turned away from him and faced the mirror. Out of the corner of her eye she watched him pause before walking back out.

Only after she heard the front door shut did she let out a sigh. If she wasn't ready to let everyone know about them, she simply wasn't ready. He'd have to be a grownup and deal with it.

* * *

Nick cursed himself for the hundredth time as he steered into the parking lot of his shop. What the hell was the matter with him?

Unfortunately he knew the answer. The man and the animal inside him wanted to mark Carly and let the world know she was his. She wasn't ready though. So why was he having such a hard time accepting it? And why did she want to hold off anyway? She might not know they were mates but she had to feel the same connection he did. Or at least something similar. The woman was absolute dynamite in his arms. There was no faking that.

He slammed his car door shut and stalked toward the front door of his office but jerked to a halt. The garish roses that had been on Carly's desk were smashed and scattered across the entrance. And he'd seen Carly throw them out yesterday—he'd been irrationally pleased she had too.

His entire body tensed at the possible implication. Why would someone go to the trouble of digging flowers out of a Dumpster? Carly had told him her ex-boyfriend had cheated on her so it was doubtful he'd do something like this. Not to mention he lived in Chicago. Or Nick assumed he did. Whoever had sent them must have done this.

The parking lot was empty, but he glanced around the surrounding area. A few cars sat in the restaurant across the street but he recognized all of them.

As he bent to gather the fallen petals, a new scent accosted him. He took a deep breath, sniffing the air. It was faint, but something foreign pricked his nostrils. There were so many surrounding smells so he focused on what was new.

He couldn't define it but it was earthy, piney, and he detected something acrid and coppery. Almost as if something had been burned recently. The only thing he was sure of, it wasn't human. Or not all human, anyway.

Nick glanced at his watch then unlocked the front door. After grabbing a garbage bag from the supply room he hurriedly gathered the crushed flowers and bagged them. As he was tossing them in the garage's oversized trashcan, Alex walked in zipping up her coveralls.

"Morning, Cousin," she said through a yawn.

"Who sent those flowers to Carly?"

She rolled her eyes. "Well good morning to you too."

"Who?"

Alex shrugged and started rolling up her sleeves. "I think it was that guy Dennis from Friday's party. I felt bad for the guy so I gave him her number."

His hands clenched into balls by his side and he knew his wolf was probably in his eyes.

She immediately held up her hands in mock surrender. "Hey, that was before I realized you were
seriously interested. I gave him her number and I'm
pretty sure he's the one who sent the flowers. I
don't know though, why not just ask Carly?"

Because he didn't want to seem like a jealous asshole.
The card had been blank anyway and Carly hadn't
seemed to know who'd sent them. He hadn't wanted to push her. Instead of voicing his thoughts, he
said, "Where do you know that guy from?"

"I don't know. I think he's one of my brother's
friends. They might have met at a club or something." She shrugged again in that typically unconcerned way of hers and he forced himself to bite his
tongue.

Nick's generation was so different it was sometimes hard to comprehend the way Alex and her
siblings acted. Inviting virtual strangers to family
get-togethers was something he would never contemplate. He made a mental note to talk to his father and Thomas about it. This kind of behavior
was going to end now.

"Don't give Carly's number to strange men anymore," he ground out.

"Jeez, I'm sorry. Let me get some coffee first then you can yell at me." She stalked past him, flipping her dark hair as she did.

Nick scrubbed a hand over his face and racked his brain. There had been something a little off about the guy at the party, but he couldn't put his finger on why. Not to mention, Nick had been more interested in getting Carly alone than talking to the man hitting on her.

His cell rang, jarring his thoughts. He answered when he saw Thomas' name. "Hey, I've been meaning to call you."

"Hey, little brother. I heard through the grapevine that you've found your mate." There was an unexpected note of sadness in Thomas' gravelly voice.

"And what grapevine would that be?"

"Who else? Mom called and she is not happy with you."

"How the hell does she even know?"

"Alex told her. I expect we'll be meeting her tonight?" Thomas asked.

"No. She's not ready to meet everyone." He hadn't had a chance to cancel with Carly yet, but if this morning was any indication, she definitely wasn't ready. It was apparent she was feeling overwhelmed by their relationship so he couldn't introduce her to the pack. Rules could be damned. If he did, he'd risk alienating her forever. He refused to lose his mate.

"She said that?"

"No. But she's human and I think I'm pushing her too hard..." He shook his head and walked across the garage toward the lobby. Carly would be in soon and he wanted to talk to her. "Listen, that's not important right now. What kind of being or creature smells like earth and fire?"

"Uh, demon?"

"No, it's definitely not that." There hadn't been a trace of sulfur in the air and the scent had been too faint. The scent of a demon was unmistakable and as a rule, they rarely visited this realm in pure form.

"Fire..." Thomas was silent for a moment, then he spoke again. "Was it almost like the forest or a forest fire?"

"Yeah. There was a piney undertone."

"Could be an Immortal."

Nick frowned. He hadn't come across an Immortal in nearly a hundred years. They were a solitary bunch and for the most part, the few he'd met were all a little unhinged. Hanging around for a few millenniums could do that to a person, he supposed. "It's possible, I guess."

Thomas snorted. "Anything's possible. Why are you asking?"

He briefly described what had happened with the flowers and was surprised by his brother's reaction.

"You need to bond with your mate as soon as possible." Thomas' words came out as a harsh, throaty order.

"Don't you think I know that?"

"I'm serious. I'm not saying he is, but if this guy is an Immortal and he's fixated on your woman, he'll stop at nothing to claim her. He won't care that she's technically supposed to be mated to someone else. Until you've marked her, she's fair game. To *anyone*."

"How do you even know this?"

Thomas sighed and Nick could practically see him drumming his fingers on his two hundred-year-old oak desk in annoyance. "Because I paid attention in history class."

"I paid attention." Sort of. When he'd been a randy pup, listening to the history of werewolves, other shifters, and pretty much all other nonhumans hadn't been high on his list of priorities. Not even close. He'd learned what he needed to know about his own kind and that had been good enough for him.

His brother cleared his throat. "Yeah, right. If this guy is an Immortal, it sounds like he might control fire, so be careful. I don't know if it's true, but I've heard they need sex to stay strong. You don't want this guy fixating on your female."

Nick inwardly cursed. He might not remember much from school, but he knew enough that Immortals could be some scary guys if they were powerful enough. He shook those thoughts away and straightened behind the counter when he saw Carly drive up. "I will."

"I don't care how you explain it to her, but you need to mate with her. The last thing our family needs is to tangle with an Immortal."

"I said I'll take care of it," he ground out.

After they disconnected, he slipped his phone into the pocket of his coveralls. He still needed time to make sure Carly was ready, but if a powerful being wanted her, it didn't look like he was going to get the chance.

From what he remembered, there were four different types of Immortals. They either controlled fire, earth, water or wind. The four elements. Some believed Immortals were somehow connected to the earth, because if they died, they turned into whatever element they controlled when they were alive. No one truly knew much about them, however. Unfortunately they were lone beings and it wasn't as if they were going to announce their weaknesses to the world.

The bell dinged as the glass door opened. Carly half smiled at him as she walked in. "Hey."

"Carly, I'm sorry about earlier." He'd felt like a dick leaving like that, knew he shouldn't have.

"Okay." Even if he couldn't smell her annoyance, it was written all over her pretty face when she tried to move past him. Her eyebrows rose haughtily when he wouldn't let her. "You gonna let me pass?"

"We need to talk."

She crossed her arms over her chest. "Fine. Talk."

He glanced toward the inside of the garage before meeting Carly's heated gaze. Most of the guys were arriving, but no one could possibly hear what he was saying to Carly. "I really am sorry about this morning."

"What exactly are you sorry for?"

"For being a jackass."

Her lips pulled up at the corners and the vise around his chest loosened. That was definitely a good sign.

When she didn't respond, he continued. "There are some things I want to talk to you about tonight..." Out of the corner of his eye he watched an oversized, overpriced SUV park next to Carly's small car.

When the man from Alex's party stepped out, Nick's entire body went into battle mode. His wolf clawed at him, demanding he protect Carly. He had to force his canines not to extend.

He could feel his bones start to shift, readying for the change. If Immortals were as dangerous as his brother said, he'd change in broad daylight for Carly and the rest of the world to see if that was what it took to protect her. Even if he didn't want to, if he felt threatened enough, his inner wolf would protect its mate at all costs. Human reasoning didn't even factor into the equation. It had been nearly a decade since he'd fought someone to the death, but if that was what it came down to, so be it.

"Why can't this guy get the hint?" Carly muttered next to him.

Her voice pulled him back to their current situation. Without looking at her, he said, "Go to the office and shut the door."

She placed a gentle hand on his arm. "Nick, I can take care of this myself—"

"Get in the fucking office!" He hadn't meant to shout, but getting Carly out of the way was all he could focus on.

Next to him she gasped, but did as he asked. As soon as the door shut behind her, Nick walked around the counter. He met the man who called himself Dennis as he opened the front door.

The man's green eyes flared an unnatural shade, but he didn't step any farther into the shop.

"What are you doing here?" Nick growled.

"I want to see the woman." His voice was filled with raw possessiveness.

"The *woman* doesn't want to see you." The fact that he didn't even refer to Carly by name riled all Nick's aggressiveness.

"Says who?" Dennis sneered.

Nick took two steps toward him until they were inches apart. "Says me. I know what you are so I'm guessing you know what I am. Stay away from her or I'll rip your fucking heart out with my bare hands." He spoke low enough so it was impossible to overhear.

Even though he didn't step back or flinch, the man's green eyes flared again and Nick knew he'd hit a nerve. If Nick remembered right, he'd have to cut off an Immortal's head or rip his heart out to kill one.

"She is not marked, lycan." His words were just as low and menacing.

Nick gritted his teeth. So the man did know what he was. "She will be."

His gaze strayed behind Nick—no doubt to the shut office door hiding Carly—before returning to Nick. A smirk played at his lips. "We will see." At that, he turned on his heel and left.

When the bell jingled overhead, Nick heard the office door fly open behind him.

Nick swiveled just in time to see Carly marching toward him. "What the hell was that?" She didn't give him an opportunity to answer as she poked him in the chest. "That macho bullshit might work on other women, but don't you *ever* talk to me like that again."

He bit back a sigh. "Carly—"

"I don't want to hear any excuses! Just because we're sleeping together does not give you the right to—"

"Carly!"

She placed a hand on her hip as she glared at him. "What?"

He cleared his throat and nodded behind her. Jimmy and Rodrigo stood in the open doorway leading to the garage, both wide-eyed and not bothering to hide their interest.

She turned then swiveled back to face Nick, her expression murderous. It was probably messed up, but seeing her riled up was insanely hot. Without another word she stalked back to her office.

"Can I help you guys?" Nick asked his two employees, neither of whom had seen fit to make themselves scarce.

"Sorry, boss. We just saw you get in that guy's face and thought something might be wrong," Jimmy said.

"If you see him here again, call the cops." It was doubtful the cops could do much to stop an Immortal, but most nonhumans didn't want to attract any unnecessary attention if they could help it. It was simply the nature of things. And it was all Nick could hope for under the circumstances.

CHAPTER TWELVE

Carly peered through the peephole of her front door and frowned. She'd managed to leave work without talking to Nick. She took a step back from the door, as if he somehow had X-ray vision. For a moment she tried to decide if she should answer. Maybe she could pretend she wasn't home.

He knocked again. "Come on, Carly. I know you're in there. I can smell you."

"Smell me?" she muttered. Grasping the door handle with one hand, she twisted the lock and jerked the door open. "What the hell do you mean you can smell me?"

To her surprise, he was smiling. Well, his version of a smile anyway. "I knew it would rile you up enough to answer the door. Your car is outside, that's how I knew you were here."

Most of her anger dissipated as she stared at him. He stood in front of her with his hands in his pockets and he didn't make a move to enter her apartment.

"Well?" she asked.

He cleared his throat. "Can I come in?"

"Fine, but only because it's humid out," she snapped.

She stepped back and let him pass, then wanted to bite back her smartass words. Arguing with him left a strange, sick sensation in the center of her gut. She might be annoyed with him, but he'd seemed genuinely alarmed when that guy from the party had shown up at work. It had freaked her out a little too, but he shouldn't have yelled at her. "Do you want something to eat?" she asked as she slid the lock back into place.

He took a few more steps into the foyer. "Sure."

"Well, my grandma brought over a shepherd's pie earlier. How does that sound?"

"I really don't care, Carly." He stopped and turned to face her. Before she realized what he was doing, his big hands had settled on her hips, his grip possessive. "I'm sorry about earlier. I shouldn't have yelled at you this morning."

"No, you shouldn't have."

"It won't happen again, I promise... Are we okay?"

"Yeah... Does everyone at work know we're sleeping together?" She'd hidden out in her office most of the day and had only come out to have lunch with Alex. And Alex hadn't breathed a word about anything.

Nick nodded, not looking very torn up about the idea. "Probably."

"At least you're honest."

He tugged her a little closer so that their bodies were touching. And there was no mistaking what he wanted. His cock pressed against her lower abdomen with insistency.

"Do you think I should let you off the hook so easily?" she murmured.

"Probably not." With one hand he threaded his fingers through the curtain of her hair and cupped the back of her head in a possessive grip. Maybe she should stay mad at him longer, but she didn't have the energy. And after she'd had time to think about it, she could tell his reaction had come from a place of fear—for her.

After the cold shoulder he'd received all day, Nick had taken a chance coming over to Carly's place. With an Immortal after her, he hadn't had much of a choice. Even though he'd wanted to wait, Nick was telling Carly what he was tonight. But first, he was going to make her come. A lot.

If he could get her in the right frame of mind, maybe she'd be more willing to listen to what he had to say. Because there was really no easy way to tell her that he could change into an animal.

Her blue eyes brightened with undeniable need as he bent his head to her neck. "You make me crazy," she murmured, a light laugh in her voice.

"Right back at you." He raked his teeth over her skin. His little redheaded vixen tasted sweet and salty. He traced his tongue across her soft neck and his cock jumped. He wanted in sexy Carly right now, but that wasn't going to happen. Considering everything he needed to tell her, she was going to get a lot of foreplay.

As he traced his tongue over her delicate skin, he could feel her moan reverberate through her throat. For a second, he managed to tear his mouth away from her. "Upstairs?" he whispered against her ear.

In response, she clutched his shoulders and wrapped her legs around his waist. Now his cock was really raring to go. Even with clothes in the way, it was like a heat-seeking rocket on a mission.

As he bounded up the stairs, Carly rolled her hips against his, making it increasingly more difficult to focus on giving her foreplay. Once they reached the foot of the bed, he stopped and she un-wound her legs from his waist.

Nick took a step back. "Strip." He was barely able to gasp the word out.

A seductive grin played across Carly's mouth as she reached behind her. She'd changed out of the restrictive skirt she'd worn to work. Now she wore a simple sleeveless summer dress the color of her eyes.

He heard the zipper unfasten seconds before the wispy material pooled at her feet. *All mine.* The two words echoed around in his head as he stared at her. Sometimes it was damn near impossible to breathe when he was in the same room with her.

She placed a manicured hand on her curvy hip. "Now what?"

"Lose those too," he murmured, motioning to her black panties.

She hooked her fingers under the thin straps and wiggled her hips as she shimmied them off.

The scent of her desire hit him like a Florida heat wave. It was thick and sensuous and he couldn't wait to taste her. "On your back."

Grinning, she shoved the comforter out of the way and spread out for him on the sheets. Gorgeous red hair pillowed around her, giving her an almost angelic quality. Nothing about her actions or the heat coursing through him was innocent though.

Carly propped up on her elbows and looked at him with an almost glazed expression. Her eyes glittered. "I want you in me, Nick."

His throat seized up for a moment. Tonight was supposed to be soft and gentle and full of foreplay.

"*Now.*" The throaty way she said it was definitely an order. When she spread her legs apart even farther, his cock pushed harder against his jeans.

That sweet raspberry scent of hers enveloped him like a drug. In seconds he'd stripped off his clothes and left a condom lying on the bed next to them. By this point, the foreplay he'd planned was a distant dream, but as long as he didn't put the condom on, he'd be able to hold off a little longer.

Nick grabbed her ankles before slowly running his hands up her inner legs. Her skin was smooth to the touch. Underneath his fingers, her body trembled and hummed with energy.

He didn't know if it was because they were mates or if her desire was so potent, but her scent was almost overwhelming. Unable to take the torture anymore he leaned forward and licked the length of her pussy.

Her hips jumped as he stroked her and his body was screaming at him to claim her. To pound into her and take everything she could give him. Then come back for more. He lifted his head for a moment and met Carly's gaze. "Tell me what you want."

"You." Her chest rose and fell rapidly.

"Say the words," he growled.

She pushed up from the bed and grabbed his shoulders with unsteady hands. "I want you to fuck me." The statement was low, almost a whisper, but that was good enough for him.

As Nick covered her body with his, Carly's inner walls clenched with need. His tongue or his fingers just weren't going to cut it. For some reason her skin was super-sensitized. Everywhere he touched her or even looked at her burned.

He settled between her legs, but didn't penetrate her. Instead, he began rubbing his cock over her pulsing clit. The quick movements sent shivers to all her nerve endings, but only increased the ache deep in her womb.

Nick zeroed in on the column of her neck and feathered demanding kisses across her skin before sucking an earlobe into his mouth.

178 | SAVANNAH STUART

Her breasts swelled under his kisses. She shuddered and wrapped one leg around his back. After the day she'd had, she wanted sex that was hard and fast. Something to take the edge off. She figured they both needed it.

She ran her hands over the bunched, tight muscles of his chest and reached around to his backside. Digging her fingers into his ass, she squeezed. Her pussy spasmed with the need to feel his cock in her. "I want you inside me, now."

"Not yet," he murmured against her ear as if this was all a game.

Nick reached between them and placed a calming hand over her belly before dipping his head to her breasts.

Using his tongue on one, he scraped his teeth over her soft flesh, circling her areola, but never directly touching her nipple. In the same moment, he cupped the other breast and leisurely ran his thumb over her hardened nub. The erotic sensations were almost too much to bear. She shifted and reached between them. Grabbing his thick shaft, she squeezed. "Get on your back."

"What?"

"You heard me," she whispered, suddenly feeling a little unsure of herself. Maybe if her voice was more forceful he'd take her seriously.

She'd never been one to take the reins in the bedroom and Nick was the most dominant man she'd ever been with. The thought of being in control turned her on more than she could have imagined. Cream flooded her pussy at the thought of having Nick at her mercy.

It was almost imperceptible, but his jaw twitched before he nodded and did as she instructed. She inwardly grinned. This had to be killing him, giving up control for even a little while.

She kneeled in between his open legs and ran her hands over his muscular thighs, savoring the feel of the corded, rippling tendons. His cock moved of its own accord, before she'd even touched it.

Unable to stop herself from grinning, she fisted his cock at the base and stroked him. Instantly a bead of pre-come formed at the tip. The small pearl glistened in the dim light.

Without wasting any more time, she bent down and ran her tongue along the underside of his shaft, starting at the base and licking all the way to the tip.

He let out a low groan and grabbed onto the head-board above him.

A few more beads of fluid came out of his small slit. She ran her tongue around the head, encircling the engorged mushroom cap. Every moan and slight noise he made, gave her more encouragement and got her even hotter. The fact that Nick liked what she was doing ensured she found pleasure in it.

Keeping his shaft firmly in her hands, she shifted lower against the sheets and briefly teased his heavy sac with the tip of her tongue. Once she'd tasted every inch of his cock, she hovered over the crown before sucking him in fully. It was impossible for her to take him all the way in her mouth, but she used her hands to stroke him as she sucked and licked.

"Fuck yeah," Nick rasped. "Just like that, sweetheart."

Nick's large body trembled underneath hers, his groans pure music to her ears. Twisting her body slightly to the left, she continued stroking him, but positioned herself so one of her breasts rubbed against his thigh. The sensation was purely erotic and she could tell it was making him crazy.

"Keep going." His commanding voice rumbled through her, made something deep inside her flare with need.

She increased her momentum, sucking him harder with each stroke. When he threaded his fingers through her hair, she knew he was close. Could feel it in the stiffness of his body.

Her lungs burned, but she kept going. She could barely hear her own sucking sounds above his harsh moans.

"I'm about to come."

The way he barely rasped out the words and loosened his grip on her head told her that he was telling her for her benefit. The message was clear, if she didn't want to swallow, now was the time to move.

She'd never swallowed before but she'd also never been with a man like Nick. Tasting him suddenly seemed like the most important thing. As she feasted on him she slackened her mouth and ever so slightly scraped her teeth against his shaft. She didn't know why, but she knew he'd enjoy it.

Just like that, his body stiffened and he exploded. As she tasted his saltiness, she continued pumping him with her fist until she'd sucked him dry.

When she raised her head and met his gaze, his eyes were glazed over in pure bliss.

"That was fucking amazing," his words were almost slurred as his head fell back against one of the pillows.

Pushing up, she shimmied up his body and straddled his waist. "I hope you're not too tired because—"

Nick cut her off as he grabbed her hips and pushed her off him. Every line in his body had gone tight. Something was definitely wrong. "Do you smell that?"

She sniffed once. "Smell what?"

Nick pushed off the bed. "Smoke and fire. It smells like—"

Carly followed suit as the overwhelming scent hit her. "I smell it too. I think it's coming from downstairs."

Nick scooped her dress off the floor. "Put this on. I think your place is on fire."

CHAPTER THIRTEEN

"Stay behind me," Nick ordered Carly after he'd hurriedly jerked on his pants.

The smell of smoke tickled his nose but if they were fast, they might be able to get out of the apartment. He carefully opened the bedroom door and a wave of smoke accosted them. He was worried more about himself than her. Humans were more fragile.

"Shit!" He slammed the door shut and hurried toward the bathroom.

"What are you doing?" Carly stood right behind him as he grabbed two towels from one of the cabinets.

He shoved one towel at her. "Wet this down."

Without questioning him, she began soaking her towel in the sink while he drenched his using the faucet in the tub. "Wring it out when you're through," he said without turning around.

Seconds later they were finished and standing by her bedroom door. "Stay low and try to breathe normally through the towel."

Carly didn't panic, but wrapped the towel around her face and was following his every move.

Nick tapped the handle with his hand and it still wasn't hot. He opened the door again and smoke billowed in immediately. Taking Carly's hand, he crouched down and they crawled toward the stairs.

It was impossible to guess where the fire started, but if he was a betting man, he'd say the kitchen. And his gut told him this was no accident.

When they reached the stairs, he squeezed Carly's hand and they slid down the first couple stairs. It was too thick to see anything. Even with his extrasensory abilities, crawling through the white smoke was like steering a plane blind.

As they inched down the stairs he realized he still didn't feel any heat. That could mean a number of things. The fire was slow spreading—though that wouldn't explain the thick smoke. Or, someone had set off some sort of smoke bomb. That would be even worse because it meant someone wanted to flush them out of the house.

If it was the Immortal, he wouldn't want any harm to come to Carly so he probably wouldn't risk burning her alive.

Nick's heart rate increased as they reached the bottom stair. They could be walking in to a trap and there wasn't a damn thing he could do about it. He took Carly's hand and placed it on the waist of his jeans. He couldn't hold her hand while they were crawling and he didn't want to lose her.

The front door was the closest, most obvious exit. A few moments later they were by the door. Despite the wet towel, his eyes were watering and he could only imagine how much Carly was suffering.

Closing his eyes, he lifted up on his knees and unlocked the door. As he opened it, a whoosh of fresh air greeted them. Under any other circumstances he would have let Carly go first, but if someone was lying in wait for them, he wasn't taking any chances.

Nick scanned the yard as they tumbled onto the front porch. He didn't see anything out of the ordinary and unfortunately he couldn't smell much. If someone was trying to trap them, the son of a bitch did a good job masking his scent. Either way, he was getting Carly the hell out of here.

Hooking his arm under Carly's, he helped her stand and walk to the middle of the yard.

She wiped her eyes and took off the towel at the same time he did. "What the hell is going on? I don't see a fire."

Smoke billowed out from window cracks and the front door of her two-story apartment, but she was right. No flames. Time to get out of here and ask questions later.

The wind shifted suddenly and all the hair on the back of his neck stood up. The leaves of the surrounding oak and palm trees ruffled and even with the dull city lights, a full moon hung high in the gray sky. "Is your grandmother home?" He hadn't seen her car when he'd arrived.

"No, it's her bunco night. Why are you whispering?" she asked, keeping her voice equally low.

"Whatever happens, promise you'll listen to me without question." He needed to see where the threat was before he got her out of here.

"I don't understand—"

Carly abruptly stopped talking as a figure emerged from around the corner of her apartment.

"Stay behind me," Nick growled as he put himself in between Carly and the man in the black trench coat. Seriously, a fucking trench coat. "Who are you?" he demanded.

The man with the dark hair and flashing green eyes kept a distance of about twenty yards between them. "My real name is Asha. Give me the woman and I'll let you live." His voice reverberated through the trees with an otherworldly growl.

"She's mine." Nick's growl was quieter, but just as deadly.

He found it interesting that the other man started to move to his left and not closer toward them. He obviously had some weaknesses. And his name. Asha? It sounded Eastern. Damn he wished he'd paid better attention in history class.

"Then why haven't you marked her, lycan?"

The scent of Carly's fear tickled his nose but he couldn't comfort her now. And he hated that. He could feel the change coming on. If anything, he was about to scare the hell out of her. Nick ignored the Immortal's question. His answer wouldn't make a difference anyway.

"Carly, start walking backward. Take small steps. When I make my move, run," he murmured under his breath.

It was impossible to know if she would follow his orders, but Nick took a few steps toward Asha. When he did, the other man's hands started to glow a bright orange. It was subtle, but Nick saw him take a step away from him. Interesting. "If you somehow manage to kill me and take my mate, my pack will hunt you to the ends of the earth. You must know that."

"She is not marked! I want the female," the other man growled, ignoring Nick's threats.

Everything around Nick funneled out until his focus was solely on Asha the Immortal. There was a flash of bright light as fire shot from the man's hand.

That was all Nick's wolf needed to change. Even if his human side didn't want to change, he had no choice in the matter. His life and his mate's life were being threatened. No matter how many times he did it, changing form hurt. Flesh tore, bones shifted and snapped, clothes ripped, and fangs extended. It was almost instantaneous.

In the background of his mind he thought he heard Carly scream, but he tuned it out.

Protect his mate. That was his only thought.

He was much stronger in wolf form and he planned to use that to his advantage. His fur burned where he'd been hit, but it was barely an after-thought.

Growling deep in his throat, a savage roar erupted as he lunged at the Immortal. Attack and retreat wasn't an option in this fight.

The Immortal would fight to the death. He went for the throat, but the other man was fast. Much faster than a human. He twisted and Nick's fangs sank into the flesh of his shoulder.

A coppery, bitter taste filled his mouth and he bit down harder, tearing through bone and tendons. A searing pain ripped through his side, forcing him to release his grasp.

Howling in pain, he fell to the earth, landing on all fours.

The stench of burning fur surrounded him, but he continued to circle the Immortal. All he needed was one opening. More than anything, he just needed to keep this guy focused on him long enough so Carly could escape.

One of his opponent's hands burned bright but the arm he'd injured hung lifelessly at his side.

A sharp, piercing scream reverberated through the air. Carly! He didn't turn because he couldn't risk it. But the Immortal did.

For a split second Asha's gaze shifted and Nick saw his opening. Using all his raw energy and rage, he lunged.

Instead of tearing through flesh, he tore through air.

A rush of wind pushed his fur back as a giant mass of black fur and sharp teeth flew past him. Before he could move, the other wolf ripped through the Immortal's throat, severing his head completely from his body.

The Immortal was dead and his mate was safe. His brain computed the thought and he collapsed against the grass. A low pain spread up his side and deep in his belly. Maybe he'd been hit harder than he realized.

Ohmygodohmygodohmygod! Carly clutched her stomach and forced the bile back. What the hell was going on?

The man she was sleeping with turned into a giant gray and white wolf-dog-looking creature, a crazy man was shooting fire from his hands, then two other black wolves showed up.

And one had just ripped the head off the fire-throwing guy. Carly stumbled once before falling on her butt. The grass provided a soft landing and she was too terrified to move. Which was probably stupid, but her entire body was trembling. She vaguely thought she might be going into shock.

Sirens sounded in the distance but she couldn't tear her eyes away from the fallen gray wolf—no,

Nick—and the other two wolves. One of the black animals stood over the gray one, licking his face and howling as if it was in pain.

The other stood over what used to be a man but was now a crumbling mass of ash and dwindling flames.

She must have made some sort of noise because instantly the two black wolves turned to look at her. When one started stalking toward her, her flight instinct flared to life and she sprung to her feet. "Uh, nice doggie—wolfie—whatever." Her voice shook as she took a couple steps back.

Instead of advancing, as she expected, the black wolf with the dark eyes started changing before her eyes. There was a cacophony of harsh breaking sounds before a completely naked man—Stephan Lazos—stood before her. Even though she'd just seen the same thing happen in reverse, she blinked a couple times.

"What..." The word barely squeaked out.

"Carly, listen to me. I hear sirens, which means someone probably saw the smoke and called the fire department. You're going to tell the police you don't know what happened, do you understand?"

She didn't *know* what happened so she wouldn't be lying. Unable to find her voice, she nodded before her gaze strayed to the other two wolves.

"Thomas is going to get Nick away from here before anyone arrives," Stephan said, as if he read her mind.

"Is Nick going to be okay?" She wanted to race over to him, but wasn't sure if she should. What if he didn't recognize her in wolf form? And she couldn't believe she was even thinking in those terms.

"He'll be fine. I'm going to stay here. I know a lot of the fire department guys and I'll do most of the talking. Just agree with me. Okay?"

No, it wasn't okay. She desperately wanted to see Nick, but… "Okay."

He turned and nodded. Almost immediately the black wolf pushed the gray one until it stood. The gray wolf turned to her and she found herself staring into familiar pale gray eyes.

Despite everything she'd witnessed, her brain was just starting to comprehend what was going on. When the gray wolf took a step in her direction, she jumped back. Guilt coursed through her at the hurt sound the animal made, but she couldn't help it. It had just been instinct, but she still felt terrible. Seeing the man she was pretty sure she loved change into a scary wolf was a twenty on the Richter scale of crazy. Even so, she hated that she'd just hurt him. "Nick..."

But he turned away from her at the sound of sirens growing louder.

Stephan shot her a desperate look, glanced toward the two animals, then back at her. "Just stay put, okay." It wasn't a question.

Before she could respond, Stephan and the wolves disappeared around the corner of her grandmother's house, leaving her behind.

Wearing her skimpy summer dress and no shoes, she nervously glanced around the yard and wrapped her arms around herself. The pile of smoldering ash had nearly dissipated.

About a minute later Stephan reappeared. This time he wore jeans, a T-shirt, and running shoes.

Before he could say a word she blurted, "Where's Nick going? Are you sure he's okay?"

Stephan rubbed a tired hand over his face. "Thomas is driving him to our parents' estate. He's... Nick is injured and he'll heal faster in wolf form."

The sirens were getting louder so she rushed on. "What exactly are you guys?"

"We're shifters. To be exact, we're werewolves. Or some people call us lycans. Not like you see in the movies though. We *do* have to shift, but we don't shift during full moons unless we want to and we don't run around like uncontrollable monsters."

"So what happened to that guy? And who was he? And what did he want?" She pointed toward the leftover ashes. Her voice rose with each syllable but she couldn't seem to stop herself.

"That guy was an Immortal. I haven't seen one in nearly a century and to be honest, I don't know much about them. They're very territorial and when he met you, he decided he wanted to keep you."

"Keep me? I'm not a piece of furniture!" she shrieked.

Stephan shrugged, and his unconcerned attitude pissed her off even more. "To him, you would have been. He would have used you up until he was tired of you. Then he'd have likely killed you."

She turned at the blaring noises. A fire truck rocketed up the driveway and men spilled from it like ants.

"Are you going to be okay?" Stephan's voice was low and reminded her a little of Nick's.

The thought of Nick hurting somewhere brought a sudden rush of burning tears to her eyes. She shook her head. No, she wasn't okay. Not even a little bit.

CHAPTER FOURTEEN

Carly checked the front of her button-down black raincoat one more time before knocking on Nick's front door. She'd been trying to get a hold of him since everything that happened Tuesday night. Thanks to a smoke bomb, her apartment was currently unlivable and she'd been forced to move in with her grandmother. The police thought it was a couple of kids playing a prank and she was happy to let them think that because she had more important things on her mind. The past couple days had been horrible and Nick hadn't been returning her calls.

It had taken some begging, but she'd gotten Alex to tell her where Nick lived. Considering that Alex had given that crazy fire-throwing guy Carly's phone number, it hadn't been too hard to convince her.

After a few moments, she banged on the solid wood door again. This time harder and louder. She still couldn't believe Nick lived in Key Biscayne. While she'd known he did well for himself, she hadn't expected him to live in such an affluent area. Only a few miles off the coast of Miami, it was like a world away. A virtual tropical paradise. Not that she cared about any of that. She just needed to know that he was okay, to see him with her own eyes—and maybe yell at him for not calling her back.

Nick's car wasn't out front but he had a garage and Alex had assured her he'd be here. Plus, there was a Jaguar sitting in the driveway. She slammed her fist against the door again. She'd had the most insane week of her life and still no answers. If he thought he could hide from her, he was out of his damn mind.

When she raised her hand again, the door flew open. An exotic-looking dark-haired, slightly older woman stood on the other side.

Unexpected jealousy shot through her veins like hot, scorching lava. "Who the hell are you?" she asked, surprised when her question came out as a shout.

Perfect brows rose in amusement as she held out a slim hand. "I'm Alisha, and you must be Carly." There was a slight accent Carly couldn't place.

Carly frowned at the woman's hand and ignored it. "Where's Nick?"

"He's on the back porch sulking. I was in the kitchen getting a glass of wine and I thought I heard some sort of racket," she said, amusement filling her voice.

Years of manners and politeness had been drilled into Carly first by her mother, then her grand-mother. In that instant, she threw all she'd learned out the window and stormed past the small woman without another word. Her three-inch heels clacked down the hard wood floor of the hallway.

Expensive pieces of art hung on the walls, but she didn't waste time admiring them. The hallway ended abruptly and she almost tripped in her shoes. To her right was an open kitchen area and to her left was what looked like a family room. Through the glass doors she could see Nick nursing a beer on the back patio.

Her eyes narrowed on his figure. She'd been worried sick about him and he was hanging out with some slut. Taking a deep breath, she hurried through the open room and slung open one of the French doors.

Nick turned at the sound and shot out of the striped lounge chair when he spotted her. He wore casual lounge pants, no shirt, and had a thick bandage running around his rib cage. "What are you doing here?"

She faltered at his harsh tone.

"Shit. I didn't mean it like that, Carly. What...well, why are you here?" he asked.

"Are you serious?" She stared at him incredulously. "I saw you turn into a wolf, your stupid brother gave me some half-assed answers before *disappearing*, everyone at work is saying you're on vacation—*which I know is a lie*—and you won't return my calls."

"You've been calling?" The hopeful note in his voice pulled at her heartstrings.

"Well, yeah, like a billion times. But it kept going straight to voicemail. I wanted to make sure you were okay." *Screw it, she'd come this far.* She crossed the fifteen-foot divide between them until they were standing inches apart. His earthy scent immediately enveloped her. God she wanted to reach out and touch him so badly.

"That night...you flinched away from me. I didn't think you'd ever want to see me again. Hell, I thought you'd be back in Chicago by now," he muttered.

"Give me a break, Nick. I'd just had the shock of my life. I saw you turn into an animal and your brother kill some other guy—who then turned to ash." Screw it, she had to touch him. She reached out and traced a finger across his stubbled jaw. "Stephan told me you were fine. Are you sure you're okay?" she whispered.

As soon as she touched his skin, he covered her hand with his. "Now I am."

Heat warmed her blood at the contact, but she shook her head. He was injured and she recognized that look in his eyes way too well. "I have a lot of questions."

"Come on." He took her by the hand and collapsed back against the chair. When he did, he pulled her with him.

She squirmed in his lap, not wanting to lean too hard against his ribs if he was badly injured. "Are you sure I won't hurt you?"

Nick let out a low groan. "You're going to hurt me if you keep wiggling around."

"Wha...oh." She immediately stilled when she felt his erection pressing against her butt.

"Why are you wearing a raincoat?"

She could feel her face redden but was helpless to stop the heat creeping up her neck and cheeks. "Because I'm only wearing a thong underneath."

His pale eyes darkened and his grip around her waist tightened, but she pulled back.

"Questions first."

He scrubbed a hand over his face. "Okay, ask anything."

"Who's the woman who answered your door?"

His lips curved up into the sexiest grin. "After everything that's happened, *that's* your first question?"

She wasn't sure what was funny about it. "Well?"

"That's my mother."

Carly snorted. "Yeah, right. Maybe if she had you when she was twelve." Instantly she slapped a hand over her mouth and cringed. What if his mother had given birth at a young age?

"Not twelve, darling." The silky smooth voice of the woman who'd answered the door startled Carly.

Carly twisted in her seat to find the woman standing two feet away. The woman was more stealthy than Nick. "I'm sorry, I didn't mean—"

She waved a fine-boned hand in the air. "You two have a lot to talk about so I am leaving. Nicolas, I'll see you tomorrow afternoon. And Carly, I know I'll see you at my Sunday brunch." It wasn't a question, but a subtle order.

She had no clue what the woman was talking about, but Carly nodded anyway. "Okay."

She turned back to Nick after the woman disappeared into the house. "That's really your mother? She looks so young."

"We age a lot slower than humans."

She bit her bottom lip and tried to formulate her words. Over the past two days she'd had a lot of time to come up with questions. Now she struggled to find her voice. "So...this whole 'turning into a wolf' is a family thing?"

To her relief, he chuckled lightly. "Yes, my entire pack—family—are shifters. Werewolves if you want to get specific."

"Even Alex?"

He nodded. "Yes, but she truly is twenty-one. She's just a pup."

"A pup? Uh, exactly how old are you?"

He cleared his throat. "A hundred and seventy."

She blinked once but pushed past it. There would be time enough later to digest *that*. "What about silver bullets? Will those kill you?"

He shifted underneath her, suddenly looking very uncomfortable. "They're more deadly than regular bullets. If a werewolf is shot with one and the silver isn't removed, we'll die within hours from poisoning."

"Wow."

"It's not something we advertise—"

She cut him off when she realized where he was headed. "Trust me, it wouldn't matter who I told, no one would believe me anyway. So, when were you planning to tell me... Or *were* you planning to tell me?" She hadn't thought about that until right then. What if he'd just wanted a quick fling—

"Don't even think I wanted an affair," he muttered.

"Wha... Can you read my mind?" she gasped, as a hand flew to her throat. Had he been able to read *all* her thoughts? She inwardly groaned. That was beyond embarrassing.

"Yes, I can." His deep voice rumbled.

"Oh my—"

"The only reason I can read your thoughts is because we're mates. And I couldn't do that until after we made love the first time. Even then, I blocked you out. Until today." He took one of her hands and threaded his fingers through hers.

"Oh, well that's...wait, mates? What does that mean?"

"Just what it sounds like. You're my mate. Once I've marked you, if you come in contact with any other shifters or nonhumans, they'll know you're taken and they'll stay away."

"What does marked mean? That man from the other night said you hadn't marked me yet. I thought you said we were mates."

"We *are* mates, but we haven't officially bonded yet. I wanted to wait until you were ready."

She didn't ask the question, and whether or not he could see her thoughts, she guessed what she wanted to know was clearly written on her face.

He cleared his throat. "When we bond, I have to dominate you, take you from behind. While we're making love, I'll bite your neck and mark you. We'll be bonded for life."

Bite her? It was a little kinky, but the thought sent a sudden rush of heat between her legs. Then another thought crossed her mind. "You said you age slower. Does that mean I'm going to grow old and you won't?"

Nick shook his head. "Once we bond—if we bond—you'll develop a similar immune system. You'll age at the same pace I do, you'll heal much quicker, and…if you get pregnant, there is a chance you'll change into a werewolf."

Her throat clenched. "A chance?"

"It's been a couple hundred years since a were-wolf and human have mated. At least within the Lazos pack. In the past, pregnant human females change when they bond with their children."

She pressed her free hand to her abdomen. That was a lot to take in at once. A hell of a lot more than she'd even contemplated before coming here. She'd never even thought about having kids.

"I don't care about children. All I want is you," he growled, his throaty words making her pussy clench.

"You've got to stop doing that."

"Doing what?"

"Reading my thoughts. It's not fair."

"You should be able to read mine too."

She narrowed her eyes at him disbelievingly. What was she supposed to do, tap into her Jedi mind control?

When he chuckled, she mock punched him in the arm. "I'm not kidding, cut that out!"

He held up a hand in surrender. "Okay, I promise."

She was silent for another moment as she tried to gather her thoughts. "I have a lot of questions. Most of them can wait until later, but a second ago you said 'if' we bond. Do you not want to bond with me?"

He laughed aloud, but the sound was harsh. "It's not about what I want, Carly. The answer is yes, but this is your choice."

More thoughts and questions assaulted her mind but she'd asked everything she'd planned. "Okay, I only have one more question. Were you just going to let me walk away from you?"

His jaw twitched before he answered. "I wasn't able to get out of bed until a few hours ago. I was coming to see you after my mother left. There's no way in hell I'd give you up without a fight, woman."

"Right answer," she murmured. Because she wasn't giving this sexy male up. Ever. Moving slightly, she spread her legs and straddled him. The past couple days had passed in a blur, but her body had been aching for his touch.

"What are you doing?" His voice was hoarse and scratchy.

"What do you think?" As she spread her legs farther, her coat pushed up higher, revealing more skin.

She started with the top button, slowly pushing it out of the hole, never taking her gaze off Nick. As his eyes locked with hers, she made a decision.

She'd come to Miami to mix things up. Of course, she'd never planned to meet a man like Nick, but she knew what her heart wanted.

There were probably a dozen reasons why this was a bad idea, but a very good one why it wasn't. She loved him. No doubt about it. The thought of losing Nick was worse than the thought of dating someone who could turn into a wolf. That realization had shifted her entire reality. She didn't care that she hadn't known him that long, it was as if he'd been part of her life forever. She wasn't letting him go.

Nick pushed her hands out of the way when she reached the third button. There were eight in all and apparently she was going too slow.

His hands shook as he practically tore the coat off. When the buttons were undone, she shrugged it off, letting it fall behind her. It was a perfect spring evening and since his place was close to the Atlantic, a continuous breeze flowed over them.

He still hadn't made a move to kiss her or touch her really. Wearing a lacy thong, she straddled him, but after he'd gotten her coat off, his hands rested gently on her thighs.

Her skin ached where he touched her and she wondered what he was waiting for. She opened her mouth to ask but he came at her fast, his mouth devouring hers with pent up hunger and need.

There was no time to catch her breath as his tongue teased against hers. This kiss wasn't tender or gentle. No, his mouth was demanding complete submission. Something she would gladly give.

Carly clutched his shoulders as he started to move. In the back of her head, somewhere in the recesses of her brain, she knew what was going to happen tonight. She wanted it and it was obvious he did too. If she decided to listen to her rational side, it would tell her things were moving too fast.

But deep down she knew she would never meet another man like Nick. Not in a million lifetimes. He'd fought a crazy Immortal for her and had been willing to die for her. He was so incredibly special and she wanted to spend the rest of her life discovering all his secrets and making him feel as amazing as he made her.

As he pushed up from the chair, her legs automatically wrapped around his waist. He might have a bandage around his ribs but he didn't seem remotely bothered as he stood and carried her. With the ease he showed, he might have been carrying a sack of feathers.

Everything around her funneled out. She was vaguely aware of walking into the house. The door made a loud, shaking sound when it shut. He must have used his foot because both hands were latched onto her ass and he was still kissing her with an unrestrained hunger.

They rushed through a living room, a hallway, then suddenly they were in a bedroom. A very masculine room with a king-sized bed. She barely had time to digest their surroundings before he had her flat on her back. The silky sheets chilled her back, but nothing could cool the heat flowing through her.

Nick teased Carly's mouth in the same way he wanted to tease her pussy. There would be no time for that tonight however. At least not the first time.

A couple days without her in his bed had been like a lifetime. His brother had taken his cell phone and he'd had no idea Carly had been calling him. He'd been wounded and disoriented Tuesday night but he remembered her backing away from him. In fear. That image had been burned in his brain but he planned to replace it with a new image.

One of her completely submitting to him.

Now that she was in his arms, he wasn't letting her go. One of his hands found its way between her legs and he pushed her barely there thong to the side. When he covered her mound, she automatically spread farther for him.

The hair covering her pussy was a darker shade of red than the hair on her head. It was so soft and inviting. He slid his middle finger in between her folds, needing to feel what was his. To claim her. She was warm and welcoming—and oh so tight.

Pushing deeper into her, he began moving his finger in and out to the same rhythm his tongue delved into her mouth. Cream and heat coated his hand. She was soaking and ready for him, but he wanted to make sure she came once before he took her the way he planned.

Carly sighed into his mouth when he slid another finger into her warmth.

Somehow he dragged his mouth away from hers. "You like what I'm doing?" he murmured, afraid to break the quiet spell of the room.

She nodded, but he wanted more.

"Say it, Carly. Tell me what you want." He loved it when she was vocal.

Her breathing was becoming more shallow so he stilled his hand, leaving his fingers embedded deep inside her, but not moving. When she tried to shift against his hand, he pulled out.

"Don't stop." Her whisper was a quiet plea.

Experiencing primal satisfaction at her words, Nick pushed back into her, savoring the way her body clenched so tightly around just his fingers. Her sweet pussy was starting to clamp in quicker contractions and he knew she was close to coming.

He was barely touching the rest of her body. His other hand grasped the back of her neck, threading through her thick hair. Their chests rubbed against each other, but he was *barely* stimulating her.

She was that receptive to his touch. The woman was like a tight little package of dynamite and he couldn't wait to see her explode.

A little flick of his thumb over her clit and she began contracting. Sweet, little contractions. He lifted his head back and watched in awe as her eyes glazed over and she reached climax. His entire body reacted in a primal manner to the sight of her like this. Nothing about his release was going to be *sweet*. It was going to be undignified and loud.

His cock felt like a steel club between his legs. Days of being denied built up inside him.

As a pleasant sigh escaped her, he grasped her hips and flipped her onto her stomach. She let out a little yelp, but she didn't struggle. Almost immediately, she pushed up on her hands and knees and looked over her shoulder at him.

Red hair cascaded down her back and over her shoulders. The look on her face was one of desire, but he needed to be sure she was ready.

"Is this what you want?" he growled. The unspoken words were there. Because there was no going back after this.

"Yes." The word wasn't a whisper. It was said with perfect clarity.

That was all he needed to hear. He lost his jeans in seconds and this time he didn't bother with a condom. He'd explain everything to her later and right now, she didn't seem to care that he wasn't getting one.

As he tried to control his breathing, he rubbed a soothing hand down her back before squeezing her hips and plunging into her. The feel of sliding into her slickness with no barrier was beyond anything he'd ever imagined.

There was nothing gentle about his hold or his thrusts. He pummeled into her like a man on death row experiencing his last fuck. He simply couldn't help it. The deepest part of him needed to claim his

woman. Make sure everyone knew she was off limits.

His heart beat like a jackhammer, ready to burst
from the cavity of his chest as he thrust over and
over. Holding onto her, his loud groans intermixed
with her quieter ones.

Leaning down, he somehow released one of his
hands and brushed all her hair to the side. It fell
over her shoulder, and the fresh scent of her sham-
poo tickled his nose. It smelled like candy. Just like
Carly, a sweet treat to be savored.

"If you're not ready, tell me now." The animal
inside told him to shut the fuck up. The animal
didn't care if she was ready, it wanted to claim what
was his. However, the man who loved her sure as
hell cared and he wanted to please her in every way
possible.

"I'm ready," she whispered.

Holding a hand against her back in an effort to
soothe her, he resumed his thrusting. From this
position, he went deeper, could feel her inner walls
closing around him.

Shadows and light danced through the cracked
blinds, bathing her in small ribbons of the glow of
the setting sun.

When he felt his release build, he held on to one of her shoulders and nipped her neck. Gently at first, then he sank his teeth into her.

She moaned, the sound one of pleasure instead of pain.

It wouldn't be too painful. At least that was what he'd heard. Just enough to pierce the neck, locking them forever. As soon as he broke through her sensitive skin, he rocketed into orgasm.

Surprisingly, so did she. Her tight pussy fisted around him as they both pushed over the edge. The muscles in his arms and legs tightened and clenched as he let out a shout that reverberated off the walls. Carly was his mate. *His.*

After one last thrust, he collapsed, falling on top of her, even as he tried to roll to the side. They lay intertwined in silence until finally she pushed at his chest with her elbow.

He dug into the recesses of his energy and moved, allowing her to roll onto her back.

"So now we're bonded?" she murmured, rolling into him and throwing her leg over him.

He nodded, wrapping his arm around her. "Yes."

"That was amazing but I don't feel any different."

You sure about that? he asked with his mind. He didn't have any way to be sure she'd understand him, but after what they'd just experienced, he took the chance.

Holy shit! I can read your mind? Her eyes widened as she stared at him.

I told you.

A mischievous grin played across her features. *I like this. Now you'll never be able to hide anything from me again.*

He chuckled and let out a satisfied sigh. Nick didn't want to hide anything from her ever again. "I love you, Carly."

The smile she gave him could have lit up the entire city. He felt the emotions pour from her and wrap around him like a physical caress. "I love you too."

EPILOGUE

Saturday Afternoon

Nick half knocked as he entered his father's study. When he walked in, he found Thomas and Stephan already waiting at the large round table where they usually held pack meetings. "Where's Dad?"

"Uncle Yannis stopped by. They're talking privately," Thomas said.

Nick took a seat in between Stephan and Thomas and glanced between his brothers. "Do we have any idea what's going to happen?"

Stephan shook his head. "So far it doesn't look as if the dead Immortal had anyone close to him, but Dad wants to take all precautions."

"Good." Nick did too. If someone came looking for the Immortal named Asha, Nick wasn't the one who would be hunted.

It would be Thomas.

Even though Nick wanted to be pissed at his brother, he understood why Thomas had delivered the killing blow. Thomas hadn't wanted Carly to see Nick kill someone and as the oldest and next in line to be Alpha, it fell to his shoulders to protect them. Whether they wanted that protection or not. Hell, he knew how lucky he was to have Thomas and Stephan looking out for him. If they hadn't already been out hunting the Immortal, things might have turned out a lot differently.

"How are things with Carly?" Stephan asked, his voice guarded.

"I was going to wait until tomorrow to announce it, but we're officially bonded." He couldn't hold back the smug grin he knew must be on his face. Last night—and this morning—was still fresh in his mind.

After a few moments of congratulatory slaps on the back, Nick turned his attention to Stephan. "Why didn't you tell me Carly had been calling?"

Stephan shrugged, but an apologetic expression crossed his face. "Sorry. I did what I thought was best. She freaked out that night and I wasn't sure what her reaction was going to be. I didn't want anything to interfere with your healing."

Nick opened his mouth to yell at him, but stopped himself from overreacting. He might have done the same thing in his brother's position. The truth was, it would take a lot to kill his good mood.

There were a lot of unknowns in his future, but he'd found his mate and he couldn't ask for more than that.

Thank you for reading Unleashed Temptation. I really hope you enjoyed it. If you don't want to miss any future releases, please feel free to join my newsletter. I only send out a newsletter for new releases or sales news.

Find the signup link on my website:
http://www.savannahstuartauthor.com

COMPLETE BOOKLIST

Miami Scorcher Series
Unleashed Temptation
Worth the Risk
Power Unleashed
Dangerous Craving
Desire Unleashed

Crescent Moon Series
Taming the Alpha
Claiming His Mate
Tempting His Mate
Saving His Mate
To Catch His Mate

Futuristic Romance
Heated Mating
Claiming Her Warriors
Claimed by the Warrior

Contemporary Erotic Romance
Adrianna's Cowboy
Dangerous Deception
Everything to Lose
Tempting Alibi
Tempting Target

Tempting Trouble

ABOUT THE AUTHOR

Savannah Stuart is the pseudonym of *New York Times* and *USA Today* bestselling author Katie Reus. Under this name she writes slightly hotter romance than her mainstream books. Her stories still have a touch of intrigue, suspense, or the paranormal and the one thing she always includes is a happy ending. She lives in the South with her very own real life hero. In addition to writing (and reading of course!) she loves traveling with her husband.

For more information about Savannah's books please visit her website at: www.savannahstuartauthor.com.